HERE THERE BE DRAGONS

Edited by H. David Blalock

Here There Be Dragons
Edited by H. David Blalock

All rights reserved. No part of this book may be reproduced or transmitted in any form or by any means, electronic or mechanical, including photocopying or recording or by any information storage and retrieval systems, without expressed written consent of the author and/or artists.

Here There Be Dragons is a work of fiction. Names, characters, places, and incidents are products of the author's imagination. Any resemblance to actual events or persons, living or dead, is entirely coincidental.

Cover illustration by Tony Kurbanali
Cover design by Laura Givens

First Printing, June 2024

Hiraeth Publishing
P.O. Box 1248
Tularosa, NM 88352
e-mail: hiraethsubs@yahoo.com

Visit www.hiraethsffh.com for online science fiction, fantasy, horror, scifaiku, and more. Stop by our online bookstore for novels, magazines, anthologies, and collections. **Support the small, independent press...and your First Amendment rights.**

CONTENTS

Stories
- 5   The Care and Maintenance of Banzai Dragons by Gregory L. Norris
- 17   Dragon's Lament by Michael P. Coglan
- 39   Stage Magic by Karen Eisenbrey
- 54   Gladys Tuttle and the Iguana Incident by David Hankins
- 75   Snowborn by Andrew Knighton
- 86   Slayer by Benjamin Spada
- 107   Come Not Between by Erica Ruppert

Article
- 120   Know Your Dragons

Poems
- 16   Born Hungry by Rachel Nussbaum
- 37   Dragon Dream by Kerstin Schulz
- 74   Voyage of the Dragon Song by Anna Dallara
- 85   Stained Glass Dragon by Katherine Quevedo
- 106   Unauthorized by Pam Ahlen

Illustrations
- 4   Fire Dragon by Brian Quinn
- 15   The Nocturnal by Sonali Roy
- 38   Dragon Tapestry by Richard E Schell
- 53   Dragon by Stephen Lillie
- 73   At Night by Angela Patera
- 119   Drakaina by Amanda Bergloff

"Fire Dragon" by Brian Quinn

The Care And Maintenance Of Banzai Dragons
Gregory L. Norris

The package arrived one week before the official declared start of Biting Fly Season. Sumner had been lucky to score one from a dealer online, and it had cost him plenty of green. *Last in stock*, the seller had proclaimed. Sumner had hit "buy now" without hesitation.

The doorbell gonged. Sumner called up the visual on his phone—deliveryman in gray uniform with full face and limb protection though none of the chompers were out yet, driven mad with hunger, their tiny, sharp teeth chattering in anticipation of chewing into the first exposed chunk of flesh, human or otherwise, their fly eyes came upon. Like all the houses on his street and everywhere else in New England, Sumner had sealed up windows, covered doors, and patched every crack into the place conceivable. Not that such extreme measures would keep biting flies out. They found ways past human defenses. Worse, there was always the certainty that at some point Sumner would be forced to go outside—for supplies, for air, or just to avoid going as mad from his confinement as the voracious menace.

He released the front door, hastened onto the sun porch, and opened the glass storm door to retrieve the package. The familiar paranoia from stepping into the open now associated with that time of year gripped him like a fever chill—curiously hot and cold in the same instant.

Sumner gripped the square cardboard box and hurried back inside despite the absence of telltale fly buzz in the day's sunny warmth. Even if the chompers hadn't started hatching, they *would* soon enough. And he'd scored perhaps the last certain defense against the misery fated to arrive.

They'd packed the treasure in dry ice. Sumner used a steak knife to slice through the heavy tape but was careful not to puncture any deeper. As he'd been instructed to in email, he stepped back, opened the plastic inner seal, and released the fog of melting coolant. Nestled in the center of the dry ice was a small black lacquered box. He lifted it out and opened the lid. Inside was a square of black velvet cloth and what appeared to be a jade and onyx marble. Fascinated, Sumner stared at the curiosity. *That* was his new banzai dragon, reportedly better than flypaper or one of those electrified paddle fly swatters?

His hand trembled, and the marble rolled to the edge of the lacquered box, nearly spilling out of it. Sumner snapped the lid shut, trapping the jewel before it could fall.

The instructions were printed on a single sheet of white paper and riddled with typos.

Place your banzai dragon in cool, dry, dark place with the box lids opens. This will allow your dragone to breath and wake up from hibernations. This should take about one week. Bonzai dragons have been bread to only feed on biting flies. Once the season is past, your dragoon will return to its nest-box and sleep. After it hardens back into its dormant state, close its box until next flies season. Repeat process then.

He'd already watched videos online, had witnessed in amazement the miracle of banzai dragons in action— tiny gemstone hunter-killers alerted to that maddening, juicy buzz, streaking out, spitting just enough fire to engulf the enemy and then devour the singed remains.

Sumner opened the cabinet, the one with the wonky hinge that never closed fully, and set the black lacquered box, opened, among the dozen jars of spaghetti sauce that were part of his stores to get him through

Biting Fly Season. He assumed it was cool, dry, and dark in there.

That accomplished, he waited.

***

He heard them buzzing past windows, and his mind translated their insect voices into screams. Someone overseas or here at home had tinkered with the DNA of *Musca domestica Linnaeus*, the common housefly, about a decade ago. Now, *Musca carnivora Linnaues* was everywhere.

Sumner's upper arms on both sides and his right shoulder bore scars from past bites—raised purple welts that would never go away. And there was also the one on his left cheek, but his beard mostly covered that ugly mark.

He attempted to smile. Across New England, ninety percent of the population went remote during the weeks when things got bad, really bad. He reminded himself that he was lucky, unlike emergency workers and those cursed souls who traveled back and forth to jobs during the chaos in order to keep the world in orbit.

Sumner was home and, so far, none of the vicious pests had made it inside. They would. He hoped he was ready.

***

Before bed, Sumner checked the banzai dragon, as he did every night on his way upstairs to the house's master suite. The jade and onyx marble hadn't altered, hadn't moved or put forth wings, a tail, or fire-breathing snout.

It's a dud, he thought. His growing worry deepened to the verge of panic. *It's dead. I paid a fortune for a dead banzai dragon!*

He returned the box to its shelf and plodded up the stairs. Not bothering to turn on the TV—every channel would interrupt scheduled programs to report on the latest impact updates from what had already been labeled the worst Biting Fly Season yet anyway, he stripped down to his boxers and crawled into bed. The covers were taking on the smell of his sweat, the house warming with both the weather outside and also its insulation. He considered turning on the air conditioner, but that was dangerous for a number of reasons. It taxed the power grid. The sound would also alert the swarms of biting flies whipped into frenzies beyond his walls, and there was always the chance that one or more of them would find a way into the house through the wall unit.

So he sweated, suffered, in the stagnant darkness of his bedroom.

Sumner rolled over and struggled for breaths that refused to come easily. He'd replaced the pillows before fly season in anticipation of rough nights. The new ones felt like concrete beneath his head. The banzai dragon had cost him a large chunk of his savings. Not for the first time, he considered the irony—one bio-engineered predator created in response to eliminate another. It would not have surprised him to learn the architects of the pest killer were the same ones who'd unleashed the pest. The popular belief was that the biting fly had escaped the lab, mated with the common housefly, started a chain reaction that—

Plink.

He heard the sound and wondered if it was a figment of his taxed and tired mind. Then the buzz sounded, and Sumner knew the worst had happened. One of them had found a way through wall and plaster and paint and was in the room.

Jumping up, he reached for the nightstand lamp. Pain exploded across the back of his hand as tiny teeth ripped through his skin. Somehow, he managed to flip the switch without knocking over the lamp. Light drove out darkness. He saw the demon latched onto his flesh along with the trickle of freshly spilled blood.

Sumner raised his other hand, intending to strike it. The biting fly buzzed off, circled, and made a dive at his face. He shrieked, raised his hands to protect his eyes, and stumbled out of bed, hearing but not seeing the monster that had made sleep on that night like so many others impossible. It was in the house, in the room, and had feasted upon him. Already, his hand stung and itched in equal misery. If he didn't kill it, there'd be more pain. And if he didn't locate where it had entered... Biting flies left a trail of pheromones in their wake like a roadmap for others to follow.

Frantic, Sumner scanned the room. He heard it, somewhere in the corner, and imagined it licking its bloodied mouth and eager for more of him. The biting fly skittered along a patch of drop ceiling, black against the pristine white. He could use the book on the nightstand, its cover presently spattered with his blood, to swat the thing and smash it to death. Sleep was a fantasy. He had to dispose of the monster before it savaged him worse.

The biting fly made a dive at him. Sumner grabbed at the book. The lamp tumbled. The bulb shorted out, leaving him in shadows. Fresh terror gripped him. He couldn't see the horror now, and it only needed his scent to locate him.

Sumner howled in the dark. Between outbursts, he heard the buzzing. The thing came near again. He swatted blindly before straightening, falling back onto the bed, wide-eyed and driven to the precipice. His eyes—if the biting fly sank its teeth into one of them, he'd go blind, he knew. It had already happened to so many others.

A thin orange light streamed across the dark space over his head. Sumner heard the biting fly scream, the sizzle, and then the crunch. A flutter of tiny wings followed.

He waited, gulping breaths and rigid until his limbs ached from their position Sumner uncurled. Elsewhere in the house, he again heard the little wings flap, a burst of controlled flame, and another shriek from a scorched chomper. Walking on instinct from the dark room, he made it to the upstairs hallway and flipped on the light. The house sat still and silent. A note of sulfur and smoldering matches drifted through the air.

Sumner entered the upstairs bathroom, ran the hot water, and dunked his injured hand under it. He located the bottle of rubbing alcohol beneath the sink and gave his wound a liberal splash. The sting dulled the building itch. One more scar would form to mark him as a combatant in the war of this new reality.

As he shut off the water and reached for a towel, something green, black, and shiny pinwheeled down onto the faux marble countertop. Startled, Sumner yelped. The banzai dragon skittered backward in response. Sumner's shock passed. He absorbed the image of his diminutive savior—the length of his pointer finger, its reticulated bat-like wings black and sprouted from its jade body. He caught the brimstone smell of its fire breath as the tiny dragon opened its jaws and licked its mouth with a forked pink tongue.

Sumner smiled. "Good to see you."

The banzai dragon eyed him and let forth with a belch. It had eaten well on that long, dark night.

***

He named it Puff and figured the title was as common to banzai dragons as "Fido" was for dogs. Over the course of the next week, any biting flies stupid enough to enter his fortress met quick demises. Puff kept constant vigil against the buzz that alerted it to one more doomed intruder. The little predator feasted, and Sumner's pulse slowed. At night, he slept.

***

Spaghetti bubbled in boiling water on the stove. The kitchen bottled the steam with an unpleasant airlessness as, outside the windows, another humid summer day played out.

Puff sat on the back of the stove above the dials, watching.

"That's not for you," Sumner said.

The banzai dragon eyed him like a tiny version of a puppy dog.

Smiling, he stirred the spaghetti, aware of the silence around them.

***

He opened the wonky cabinet door that never fully closed. His banzai dragon rested on the square of black velvet curled up like a dozing cat. Seeing him, Puff unfurled, stretched, and yawned.

"Hey, buddy," Sumner sang.

The banzai dragon puffed up, extended its wings, and shook—according to a video he'd watched, a happy response.

"I might get through this yet," Sumner said.

The outside world continued to struggle with sanity during the annual blight. He wondered how anyone without a loyal banzai dragon could come out of it with their minds intact.

***

He counted eighty-seven kills, updating the totals in a little notebook. Eighty-seven instances of biting flies biting their way into his house, and eighty-seven biting flies singed to a crisp and devoured by Puff, his banzai dragon.

Then the nights cooled, and the days renounced their humidity. The fly season was nearly over. Soon, it would be time to remove plastic and tape from windows and doors. Puff would go hungry and, as was the nature programmed into it, the banzai dragon would curl up, hibernate, desiccate, and slumber. It was the same principle for amaryllis, narcissus, and other flower bulbs. After they bloomed one year, you cut them back, put them to sleep by not watering them, and then, next season, a hearty dose of liquid refreshment and they were back.

Sumner waited for Puff to sleep.

After the first killing frost, he took down the window plastic and unbarricaded the doors. A peek into the cabinet revealed his little champion circling in place, looking restless, hungry, and vexed.

"Go to sleep," Sumner urged.

A week after that, he saw a big, gray moth fluttering through the bedroom as he read his book. Summer was over, and things that lived outside were sneaking in to stay warm. It happened every autumn, first with moths and then spiders and field mice.

A thin streak of orange flame shot across the air above Sumner's bed. Even before the moth dropped, its wings incinerated, Puff had it in its jaws.

***

For the first time since the beginning of Biting Fly Season, Sumner readied to leave the house. He was down on everything—food, paper products, and, more so, the ability to stand being trapped within the same rooms. The geometry of his surroundings had nearly driven him mad.

It was always the same that first time outside. *Release Myopia*, they called it. A version of the same psychological malaise prisoners experience following long incarcerations mixed with a splash of Stockholm Syndrome and old-fashioned paranoia. The next four steps past his front door took conscious effort. At any second, he expected pain to erupt from some exposed patch of skin. But no telltale fly buzz greeted his ear. From somewhere close by came the reassuring sound of traffic, a reminder of the sane world.

Early autumn sunlight warmed his face. Sumner indulged in a moment of thanks. He closed his eyes, tossed back his head, and breathed in a deep breath of the crisp New England air. The chaos was over for now, and he'd survived it. Opening his eyes, he greeted the world as though seeing it for the first time.

Wind gusted through the trees. The maple near the driveway showed its first hint of butter-yellow color in some leaves. As Sumner luxuriated in his freedom, a tiny bird darted through cloudless sky the color of comfortable denim and made for the maple. Sumner tracked it. The bird—what he assumed was a finch—sang, and its joyous music matched what he felt.

The happiness proved to be brief. Something jade and black shot past Sumner and toward the maple. He watched, horrified, as a thin gust of flame surged forth, engulfing the finch in mid-song. As it dropped, its wings flapping inelegantly, Puff jumped on it and began to devour the much-larger kill.

"No," Sumner said. "No!"

The front door, he discovered, no longer closed properly as a result of the annual barricades and was how his banzai dragon had gotten out.

He picked up Puff as it choked down the last of its prey. The diminutive predator bucked against his grip and punished Sumner with a tiny jolt of flame. Howling, Sumner released Puff, shook out his hand, and realized the banzai dragon now looked twice its former size.

***

At night, in the dark, Sumner heard the dragon flapping its wings as it dove at unsuspecting prey and the sizzle of its killing flame breath. In the morning, there were char marks on walls, furniture, and floors. The living room's love seat bore a crunchy black burn pattern of singed microfiber at its center.

Before long, one of those fires would ignite and spread, he knew. The videos all preached the slim chance that a banzai dragon's flame-venom igniting an owner's house was close to zero. But they also had promised that Puff would enter hibernation stage after fly season ended, and that was a month overdue.

He approached the coffee maker, intending to brew a strong pot, and noticed the half-eaten, singed remains of a mouse on the counter. Time fell off its usual track of seconds and minutes, making one seem like the other. He opened the cabinet. Puff slumbered atop the square of black velvet in the open lacquered box. Now, his banzai dragon barely fit into its home. Two legs spilled out of the box.

"Go to sleep," Sumner whispered. *"Please..."*

The banzai dragon opened one eye and studied him, and, Sumner realized, all illusions about loyal, happy puppy dogs were missing from that stare.

***

Sumner pulled the blanket up to his chin. Outside the bedroom's windows, a stiff November wind blew around the eaves and moaned in a disembodied specter's voice.

Claws scrabbled across the floor. Sumner froze. At first, he worried an animal had gotten into the house—a cat or an opossum. It sounded that big. He tracked its steps from the hallway to the master bedroom's threshold. His heart galloped inside his ribcage.

How could something that big find its way inside through closed windows and locked doors? Then the terrible knowledge registered. It had because it had been inside with him all along.

Thawing, Sumner reached toward the lamp on the nightstand. But before he flipped the switch, the room lit, orange and vibrant, the glare originating from near the foot of the bed where the animal crouched. Then Sumner's pain caught up, and he screamed.

"The Nocturnal" by Sonali Roy

Born Hungry
Rachel Nussbaum

When the dragon slithered out of his egg
He licked each drop of yolk off the shell
Even just hatched he was so hungry
And hunger for dragons is different
From any other living thing on Earth
Their hunger grows with their heart

The hatchling's mother soon fed him
And he picked each charred bone clean
He slept on a pile of hooves and bells
And growled out at the mouth of his cave
Down at the lights in the village below
Coveting everything he couldn't devour

In time his shadow eclipsed the castle
His fire melted rock and cooked knights
He plucked the King's crown and rings
off what was left of his smoking bones
Now he glares up from a mountain of gold
Dreaming of the day he can swallow the sun

Dragon's Lament
Michael P. Coglan

Need drove her. It pushed her up the sheer walls of the mountain. It quieted the pain in her bad knee as she climbed into the icy heights of the peak.

Diana's normal route to the valley was nowhere near as arduous or dangerous. It was also several days longer than her current path. Days she and her people didn't have.

She came to a ledge wide enough to lie down on and took the opportunity to rest. Bitter wind howled around her as she stretched her legs and flexed her fingers. She needed those to be nimble when she reached her destination. She looked out over the land, barely able to make out the red painted wooden roofs of the several dozen buildings in her village far below.

Diana pulled the scrap of parchment from her pocket and began to read it for what was likely the hundredth time. She knew it by heart, but she wanted to see it written in Quaid's hasty yet bold hand.

Dearest Diana,

The day we have all feared for so long has come. I told you that I would never make this request of you, but I'm afraid that I cannot keep that promise, like so many others that I made to you. We need Coynera. We need you. I need you.

I believe our forces can hold them at the Sunrise Pass, but I don't know for how long. Please, hurry.

Forever yours,
Quaid.

The implications of his letter were terrifying, but as scared as she was, she could only think about Quaid. It was the first time she'd heard from him in ten years. She hadn't believed the messenger when he'd first arrived in the village and yelled that the great general had sent word to the Dragon Minstrel. Hope followed the disbelief, but that hope had been dashed when she'd seen the messenger's disheveled appearance and the froth on his horse's mouth. He'd ridden hard, without stopping, from the front lines of the war in the east. She'd known then that Quaid's message was not going to be one of apology or to tell her that he was finally coming home. It would be one of urgency and utmost desperation.

Feeling that same desperation, Diana readied herself to continue her climb. She adjusted her small pack and cinched her belt around her cloak to keep it from billowing in the wind. She knew that this next leg of the climb would be the last, but also the longest.

In her youth she'd gone this way for fun. She'd loved the view of the plains below and the feeling of the wind in her hair. She also hadn't wanted to take the extra time to and from Coynera's valley. She'd had things to do back in the village. She'd had Quaid waiting for her.

Memories of their time together flooded her mind unbidden as she moved from one rocky handhold to another. She remembered practicing on her viola beneath a tree as he swung his training sword in time to her music. She remembered long days spent in the sun and cool nights spent in his embrace. She could still picture the joy on his face when she'd been selected to be the next Dragon Minstrel.

But then she also remembered the arrival of the army recruiter. She remembered the tears on both their cheeks as they shared one final kiss before he left with the other men. She remembered his promise to always write and one day return, a hero to their people. To win the war and become worthy to be husband of the Dragon Minstrel.

Tears ran down her cheeks now, just as they had all those years ago. They were cold against her skin, but she didn't stop to wipe them away. She pressed onward and upward.

He'd kept his first promise for a time, but the letters grew less frequent over the years until at last they stopped altogether. She used to ask after him to travelers and returning soldiers, but she, too, eventually stopped.

She finally reached the peak of the mountain and set about making camp for the evening among the trees. The sun would go down soon and traveling the mountains in the dark was treacherous.

The small fire illuminated her long fingers as she held them up for warmth. The skin on her hands was rougher now than when she'd last touched Quaid. Would he even recognize her now? There were times she didn't recognize herself when she looked in her mirror. She felt as though her face hadn't changed much, but her hair was more silver now than the chestnut brown it had been in her youth.

Would she recognize him? What would he look like now? She imagined him as very much the same as she'd last seen him, but with gray peppering his black hair and perhaps a scar on his cheek. And more worry in his pale blue eyes with the weight of responsibility behind them.

Diana rose the next morning as soon as there was enough light to see by. This side of the mountain was less steep than the other, but was densely forested, making the progress feel just as slow. Her right knee ached so she kept an eye out for a fallen tree branch suitable to use as a walking stick. She'd left her good one back home, knowing that it would be hard to carry on the initial climb.

She reached the valley as the sun passed directly overhead. The trees gave way to a stone outcropping, jutting out above a valley nestled between the mountains. She could see the tops of the trees below and a small lake in the distance. This place always took her breath away.

It wasn't just the view, with snow capped mountains above and lush forest below. It was the sound. This valley, which bore no name, was dead silent. No bird chirped, no squirrel rustled in the underbrush, and somehow no wind blew. Diana still didn't know if the mountains protected the valley from the wind or if it was another effect of the valley's lone occupant, but she didn't care.

When she'd first come to the valley, she'd found the silence unsettling. Over the years, however, she'd come to view it as a painter views a blank canvas. With no ambient noise to contend with, her music was able to ring out across the valley in its purest form.

She breathed in the sweet scented air and removed her pack. She'd traveled light, carrying minimal provisions and only a thin bedroll. What had taken up most of the space in her pack was her viola. The sound of the clasps releasing on the wooden case echoed in the valley below, signaling that she was going to begin soon. She removed the instrument, made of polished maple wood, and set it beneath her chin. She closed her eyes and let the silent stillness of the valley envelope her.

Diana slowly pulled the bow along a string. A single low note surged into the valley. A warm, welcoming tone announcing her presence. She stopped playing and waited for a response. Just as the echoes of her own greeting faded into the distance, she heard Coynera's response, equally low, but infinitely more powerful. The note boomed, more like a gigantic trumpet than a viola.

Hello, it said.

Diana didn't hear the word so much as feel it, just as humans didn't hear the meaning of music, they felt it in their souls. She was the Dragon Minstrel, capable of interpreting the musical language of her people's dragon.

More trumpeting, now with a variance in notes and an inquisitive melody.

You're early, Diana. Why?

Diana's job was to keep the dragon, Coynera, happy. She made monthly journeys into the mountains to visit the majestic creature and engage it in musical conversation. She had last visited only one week prior.

Diana played. She shifted to a higher octave, but played slowly, drawing each note out before beginning the next.

I'm sorry, but we need your help, she played. Now that the conversation had begun, both human and dragon continued their songs uninterrupted, but alternated playing the lead parts.

I am not your pet, human, came the reply in a gravelly note. The vibrations shook the ground beneath Diana's feet.

Of course not, Diana replied quickly. *But you are my friend, are you not?*

The notes hung in the air, wafting through the air and Diana could sense Coynera hesitating.

Yes, the dragon replied in a soft tone. *But what help can I provide?*

It was Diana's turn to hesitate. She'd had the entire journey here to think about how exactly she'd make the request, but her head had been too filled with thoughts of Quaid. She moved into a minor key, playing a mournful tune.

Einor, the kingdom to the east, is attacking my people. We are dying.

Coynera's tune changed, the notes now carried derision. *And what does that have to do with me?*

I am your friend. My people are your friends. We have played for you for generations.

Are you trying to control me, human? The trumpeting was accompanied by the sound of something crashing against the stone of the mountains. A drumming in time with the horn that shook the entire valley. Diana knew that Coynera only added percussion when especially angry.

Coynera was always wary of being controlled. Dragons love music, it's the reason that dragons and humans were able to communicate and coexist, but they are also susceptible to its influence. A sufficiently powerful song could be used to sway the thoughts and emotions of a dragon much in the same way that hearing a favorite song might raise the spirits of a melancholy human.

Diana changed her song to more perfectly match the rhythm of Coynera's, allowing it to be overpowered and changed by the dragon's in a sign of reverence.

I will never control you. When I first became the Dragon Minstrel of De'Coyn I swore that to you.

You would not be the first Minstrel to promise as such and go back on their word. The pounding drums continued.

But have I?

The drumming faded and the rhythm slowed, no longer angry, but cautious.

Not yet, the dragon relented.

And I promise I never will. Diana changed to a sharp key, preparing to deliver the worst of the news. *I won't, but others of my kind are. The enemy is bringing a dragon to the battle and I don't believe that it is willing.*

Coynera's response burst across the valley. A single long note, both angry and mournful. Diana could not translate the music into words in her mind, but she didn't need to. It wasn't meant to be words, it was pure anguish. Humans were committing what Coynera held to be the most terrible of sins against one of her kind.

Tears fell down Diana's cheeks as the emotions washed over her in waves of sound and Coynera's pain began to flow through her. She played on, accompanying the note as it echoed in the valley, as it reverberated on itself over and over again before cresting the mountainous peaks and spreading out into the world.

Diana felt a rumbling in the stone beneath her. At first it was only a minor tremor but it quickly grew to the point of nearly knocking Diana from her feet. She had to stop playing in order to steady herself. The trees on the far side of the valley began to swing wildly as if blown by a tempest.

Coynera erupted from behind a ridge. The dragon was larger than every building in Diana's village combined. She found it hard to believe that the creature could hide in the valley as easily as it did. Coynera soared upward with a flap of massive, leathery wings.

Scales glistened like silver coins reflecting a sunset; vibrant red near the spines protruding from the dragon's back, and the orange of an autumn flame on the belly. Coynera's body was shaped like a horse, but the limbs were far thicker and ended in massive eagle claws. A graceful neck led to a square head surrounded by gently curving horns of various lengths. The last part to emerge was the dragon's tail, nearly as long as the rest of the body and tipped with spikes matching the horns on the head.

Seeing Coynera filled Diana with equal measures of terror and awe. The dragon defied all that she knew of the natural world. It was a legend come to life, even to a Dragon Minstrel.

The massive creature swooped down to the valley floor below Diana's outcropping, tilted its head back, and opened its mouth, revealing sword-like teeth. A song issued from the cavernous jaws and Diana knew what she needed to do.

***

Word came to Quaid as he fought at the battle center that the left flank under his lieutenant commander Gilbert was buckling. His army of 9,000 strong had been divided into three contingents to better take advantage of the terrain. He personally commanded the center, Gilbert on the left and Cohen on the right.

Quaid stepped back from the fighting, letting his personal guard surge around him to close the gap, a blur of gleaming red armor pushing against the wall of forest green that was the enemy. Once safely disengaged, he ran to the forward command base where a young man saluted his approach.

The messenger pulled a roll of paper from his satchel and held it out for Quaid to see. It was a map of Sunrise Pass with their battle plans drawn on it. Quaid stroked his graying beard with his left hand, his sword still held firmly in his right, as he looked over the markings and arrows indicating the disposition of his forces.

It made sense that Cohen's company were holding firm. They had a sheer cliff to their right flank and Quaid's own troops to their left. They were in the best position in the pass. The left flank was always going to be trouble. That was why he'd given the left flank to commander Gilbert. If anyone could hold that flank, he could.

It seemed that no one could then. At least, not alone. His thoughts drifted to Diana and the letter he'd sent a week ago. Had she received it? Had she read it? Would she come?

"Have Cohen send 1,000 men to aid Gilbert," Quaid said, his thoughts returning to the battle at hand. "We'll try to push the center forward to give them a better path."

The messenger quickly rolled up the map and began pulling out the appropriate signal flags. Quaid turned his attention back to the battle.

The sights of war had never bothered him. It was gruesome and filthy, sure, but he'd taught himself long ago to see everything tactically. Every soldier was a piece on the board that could be directed.

It was the sounds that bothered him. War was so very loud and chaotic. Men didn't fight silently and stoically, they shouted with exertion and screamed in agony. Weapons and armor clanged like a thousand blacksmiths all hammering at their works at once. If he moved away from the press of the battle itself, he would still hear the moans and wails of the injured and dying.

He longed to hear music. Something with structure and rhythm. At night, some of the soldiers would sing or play small instruments they'd brought with them from home, but none of them were true musicians. Not like Diana.

Again, his thoughts returned to his lost love. He remembered her practicing every day since the day they'd met. He remembered the way she'd listen to the ambient sounds and play in time with the world around her, giving an order to the randomness of nature.

He shook his head and returned his focus to the present moment. He needed to lead his men in a charge to create more space for Cohen's men. He heard the order already making its way among the men but he strode forward to lead it himself. He always led the central company himself, even against the recommendations of his advisors. His men needed him on the ground more than they needed him in a tent on some faraway hill waving signal flags.

This maneuver would have to work. Sunrise Pass was the last defensible position between the enemy and the capital. If they failed here, the war would be as good as over.

The war had been raging since before he'd been born. In the early years, there had only been little skirmishes along the border between De'Coyn and Einor, but ten years ago, Einor had escalated. They mounted full scale assaults and began seizing entire towns as they cut their way westward. Now, with Quaid's homeland a mere fraction of what it had once been, they were on the verge of losing everything.

Quaid clapped his men on the shoulder as he moved forward. He shouted words of encouragement as they lined up, ready to push forward with renewed vigor. They cheered as he passed them, emboldened by his presence. He took his place at the head of the central formation and raised his sword, the lowering sun glinting off the steel.

He pointed the blade forward and shouted, a deep, incomprehensible battle cry. The men around him charged. They flowed between their brothers, who'd already been engaged with the enemy, and poured forth as a sea of crimson. Quaid felt the enemy line buckle and then give, moving backwards towards the mouth of the mountain pass.

Once there were no Einor soldiers nearby, he risked a look behind him to see if Cohen's men had begun to move. He saw the orange banner flying north and then east behind them. It was working.

The battle continued that way for a time, with his army holding the line. Quaid was certain that they'd be able to hold out until the enemy retreated for the night to rest until attacking again in the morning.

Then he heard it.

Drums echoed in the little valley, beating a quick and angry rhythm. It wasn't the rhythm of signal drums or marching drums. This was music, unlike any music Quaid had ever heard, but unmistakably music. He moved back to a hill that they'd just pushed past and looked out over the battle lines.

Approaching from behind the enemy troops was a massive platform, pulled by four oxen taller than any of his men, with horns longer than spears. On the platform was a group of drummers. In the front corners were two smaller drums beating out quick patterns. Across the center there were three large drums standing with their heads facing up, drummers striking downwards in time with one another. Behind them a larger drum stood on its side, two drummers playing a deep baseline on both sides.

The resulting combination was a cacophony of sound that at first seemed as chaotic as the battle but with an odd, terrible structure to it. An angry song that only put more thoughts of violence into the minds of all who heard it.

Quaid clenched his teeth as anger seethed within him. It was actually happening. He'd read the scouting reports over and over, but some part of him had refused to believe. Not since the dark days had anyone purposefully enraged a dragon to set loose on their enemies, but these monsters were about to. The legends said that a single dragon could wipe out an entire army in moments. That they were fire and death incarnate.

Nothing else mattered if they couldn't stop the music. Quaid signaled the nearest group of archers to take the drummers out, but the arrows were turned away by a curtain of metal, like a fine chainmail, that hung from the cage surrounding the platform. He shouted to his men to attack the drummers with everything they had even as he knew it was in vain. The platform was still far behind the enemy line. There was no way they could stop what was about to happen.

It came from the right flank. A crashing sound announced its arrival, like the beginning of an avalanche. A single clawed hand gripped the top of the sheer cliff face above Commander Cohen's men, each talon larger than a horse. Rising into view above it came the wicked, reptilian head, covered with dark green scales and rimmed with black horns.

Quaid's mind reeled against his own eyes as he struggled to comprehend the creature. Its size alone was unnatural, but it exuded a terrible grace. It was a beautiful nightmare come to life to destroy everything that Quaid loved.

From its perch atop the cliff it roared, a hateful thunder. Men on both sides dropped their weapons to cover their ears. The pace of the drumming quickened. Quaid could barely hear it, but he felt it as the waves of angry percussion spread across the battlefield.

The dragon arched its long neck back then shot its head down towards the humans at the base of the cliff. Fire poured from between its jaws. Quaid felt the heat hundreds of yards away. Those within the initial blast area didn't have time to scream, they were simply gone. The remainder of Cohen's company, nearly two thousand men, was erased from the earth in a single moment.

They were doomed. All of them. Not just the kingdom of De'Coyn, all of humanity. If this kind of force existed in the world there was no stopping their inevitable destruction by it.

The dragon flapped green and black wings and launched into the sky. It arched to the east and turned back towards them.

As the dragon approached, Quaid heard another song faintly on the wind. It was light in contrast to the violence of the drumming. It filled Quaid with peace and hope. Perhaps it came from the beyond, welcoming Quaid into eternity. Quaid didn't particularly care where it came from, he was just happy to feel something other than terror.

The dragon opened its mouth as it drew close and Quaid could see the hot orange glow in its throat as it prepared to unleash unholy fire onto his men. He stood up straighter, wanting to face the afterlife proudly.

***

The first hour of riding on the dragon's back had been terrifying, but Diana had slowly figured out the best place to sit that would keep her stable. She now rested between two spikes directly above Coynera's shoulders and had lashed herself there with some rope from her pack.

Diana saw smoke rising in the distance and knew that they were close. They'd flown from Coynera's valley to the Sunrise Pass in only a few hours when that journey would take nearly a week on horseback. It still might not have been fast enough.

The valley came into view. The red clad De'Coyn armies were lined up on the west end, desperately holding the pass against the sea of green that was the Einor army to the east. Flying above the green army was their dragon, green and black and terrible. It was bigger than Coynera and had a more wicked look to its spikes and horns, but it was still unnaturally graceful as it moved through the air.

Diana saw the flames against the southern cliff face and the dragon's open mouth.

We have to stop it from breathing on them, she played to Coynera in a light, hopeful rhythm. Coynera's song didn't turn into words of agreement, but their flight path shifted to aim directly at the enemy dragon.

They collided with the force of a sudden storm. The green dragon's fire burst into the sky as it rocked backwards. It turned and arced away from them.

Diana spotted the drummers and noted that Einor had an entire troop to play for their dragon, whereas De'Coyn had only one Dragon Minstrel. She wondered if having more than one musician made it easier for them to control their dragon, but her attention was quickly drawn back to the present.

I'm going to kill the human drummers! Coynera roared. Diana felt the red dragon's anger and was going to agree, but she saw the green dragon turning back towards the De'Coyn soldiers on the north side of the pass.

No, we have to keep their dragon occupied. Let our army take care of their drummers. Besides, our people are too close to the platform for you to attack it without endangering them as well. Diana's song was high pitched and pleading. She couldn't let her people die.

Coynera growled, but relented, banking sharply north.

I will not kill this dragon, Coynera sang in growly tones. *It is not its fault, it's those wicked humans'.*

I know, Diana replied. *But the humans can fight humans. They cannot protect themselves from the dragon.*

***

Quaid watched in awe as the two gigantic creatures clashed. He felt the force of their meeting like the beating of a drum. The green dragon's fire passed mercifully overhead before the two dragons parted.

Quaid looked at Coynera, with red and orange scales matching the armor of his troops, or he supposed it was the other way around. The red and orange dragon was smaller than the enemy dragon, but was still massive.

He wondered where Diana was. Could she be riding Coynera somehow or was she still back in the village, having sent the dragon alone? He wasn't sure which one he'd prefer; for Diana to be safe at home, or to have the chance to see her again, even here, at the end of all things.

His time for rumination was short. He didn't know exactly how the Dragon Minstrel connection worked, but he knew it was based on music, and he knew where the enemy music was coming from.

He began shouting to his men, urging them to pick up their weapons.

"Men of De'Coyn!" he cried. "Einor brought a dragon, but we have one of our own! While the two titans fight each other in the sky we can still fight the battle here on the ground. They're controlling the dragon with those drums. If we take those out then Coynera can drive the dragon away. To the platform!" He raised his sword and the men around him cheered.

They could do it.
He hoped.

***

Coynera flew past the green and black dragon, trying to draw its attention from the humans below, but it remained focused on the clumps of red armored soldiers.

We have to attack it, Diana played.

No! Coynera trumpeted.

You don't have to kill it, but you must distract it enough that it doesn't hurt the humans, Diana pleaded with the dragon.

Fine, the dragon sang a low note.

They turned in the air again, approaching the green dragon from above as it swept down to claw at the humans. Diana could hear the angry drumming of the enemy musicians above the rushing of the wind.

Coynera grabbed the neck of the green dragon and turned to fly upwards, pulling it away from the troops on the ground. It turned in midair, now face to face with Coynera as they flew, and raked its claws at Coynera's snout. The smaller dragon let out a wail of pain and kicked out with its rear talons, aiming for the green dragon's belly.

The two colossal beasts began to twist and writhe in the air as they snapped and clawed at each other. Diana clung to Coynera as best she could and continued to play a song of encouragement, quick and triumphant. Diana lost sight of the battle below them, but could still hear the drumming.

The green dragon got a hold of Coynera's neck with its front claws and clamped its jaws down on it. Coynera let out a cry of pain so visceral that Diana could feel the teeth like they were sinking into her own flesh.

To this point Diana had kept her songs encouraging but light in tone, she didn't want to add to the violence of the drums, but she was beginning to think that Coynera needed more than that. Diana shifted her position on the viola's neck and began to play a new tune, faster and more persistent.

Diana was careful to not take over Coynera's mind. Her emotional link with the dragon allowed her to feel the line between encouragement and control and she made sure to stay on the right side of it, however, she was getting closer to control than she'd ever been before.

Coynera bit into the green dragon's own neck and tore free a chunk of flesh. The green dragon howled and released its grip on Coynera. The red dragon shot away from the larger one and launched a single blast of fire. The ball of flame burst against the green dragon's face, but it was unfazed.

Your humans are working too slowly, Coynera crooned.

Give them time.

We don't have time!

A stream of flame lanced through the sky and struck Coynera in the chest. Coynera was blasted backwards and fell from the sky, crashing into the mountainside above the pass. Dirt and rock flew out from the impact.

***

"Push, men!" Quaid shouted amid the sounds of the battle raging around him. He'd sent out signals for the entire army to make for the platform. Holding the line across the pass was no longer their primary objective. They could get surrounded so long as they made it to the platform.

They were close, but a forest of green spears still stood between Quaid and the platform.

He looked up to see the two dragons locked in a vicious battle. They spun about one another, snarling and snapping. He hoped that taking out the drummers would help Coynera.

Quaid screamed orders and words of encouragement to his men as he hacked his way through the enemy lines, but it wasn't enough. There were too many of them. He feared that their only hope was that Coynera could defeat the green dragon.

He felt a tremor and looked up to see Coynera fall into the northern mountain. The green dragon quickly landed on top of the red dragon and began to claw at it in time with the drumming.

That damn drumming. Why couldn't he get it to stop?

The green dragon unleashed another gout of flame directly onto Coynera. He had to squint against the brilliance of the dragon fire. The green dragon let out a roar of triumph and took to the air once more, this time alone and coming for Quaid's men.

***

Diana opened her eyes slowly, unsure of what she'd see.

She'd been thrown from Coynera's back when they'd hit the ground, her rope snapping, but she had remained sheltered beneath a wing when the green dragon had followed them. The attack had been brutal.

She crawled over to her viola, remarkably intact, a few feet away.

Are you alive? She asked with a hesitant note.

Coynera didn't move for a moment, but eventually let out a wheezing response.

I think so. Do we still need to fight?

Diana stepped out from under Coynera's wing and onto the charred mountain side. She saw the green dragon on its path towards the remaining De'Coyn troops still pushing towards the platform.

I'm not sure, Diana played a sad note. *We might be too late. My people are all going to die.*

Diana felt Coynera shift beside her.

No, they won't. The dragon stood up shakily. *You kept your word. Through the battle you encouraged me, but my decisions were always my own. You are a true friend and worthy of the title your people have bestowed upon you. We will save them, together.*

A claw wrapped around Diana's waist and lifted her onto the dragon's back once more. The scales were blackened and peeling, exposing charred flesh. Diana had wondered if dragon hide was fireproof. If it was, it wasn't fireproof enough for the inferno that the green dragon had unleashed.

The dragon flapped its wings once, but the movement was slow and weak. They remained on the ground. Diana took up her viola and began to play a song of battle and victory.

Coynera flapped again and this time the ground fell away beneath them. The flight was shaky and uneven, but Coynera kept them aloft. Diana saw the glow from the green dragon's mouth, then the fire came out. It poured onto the ground like a waterfall of death. Diana could feel the heat and hear her people dying.

Diana played faster and Coynera responded.

Thank you.

The two dragons once again collided. The force of Coynera's tackle pushed them both away from the armies and into the sheer southern cliffs. Their impact shook the earth and loosened the stones above. As the dragons came crashing down, so did the mountain.

***

Both armies stopped fighting as the mountain came down on top of the dragons. The men on the southern flank rushed to get away from the falling boulders and the flames from the green dragon's first assault were put out by the rockslide.

The mountain pass grew silent as the last rock finished its tumble. Even the drumming had stopped. All looked on, dumbstruck, waiting for some sign if either dragon had survived.

Quaid started moving towards the wreckage. Somehow he knew that Diana had been with Coynera during the battle. She wouldn't have stayed back in the village. But that meant that she'd also likely have been with Coynera when...

The grinding of stone against stone began to echo in the pass. A murmur spread among the human armies. Quaid stopped in his tracks.

Stones fell away from the pile and a red scaled head emerged from the rubble.

A cheer rang out from Quaid's men as they recognized their savior. The Einor army quickly turned to flee, abandoning Sunrise Pass rather than facing the dragon who defeated their own.

Quaid ran towards Coynera as it continued to unbury itself.

Its massive head turned towards him and their eyes met. Its eyes were larger than he was tall, but he saw within them ancient wisdom and deep emotions. Coynera extended a red scaled hand and resting between the claws was a woman with silver and chestnut hair clutching a viola to her chest.

***

Diana looked up to see a soldier with gray flecked hair rushing towards her. She climbed out of Coynera's hand and stepped into the man's embrace. She recognized Quaid's warmth the instant he touched her, and threw her arms around him. They stayed that way for a long moment. Diana only released Quaid when she heard Coynera shuffling rocks behind her.

They turned to see the red dragon lifting boulders to reveal the face of the green dragon. The men stepped back, nervous that the dragon would wake and attack them again. Coynera bent low and sniffed at the green dragon, nudging it with her snout.

It remained motionless.

The red dragon lifted its head high and let out a wail of unbearable anguish. One didn't need to be a Dragon Minstrel to feel the pain that cry carried. The song swept through Sunrise Pass and none who heard it were unmoved.

Diana saw tears running down Quaid's cheeks, and she turned to find that every soldier was openly weeping, feeling the dragon's emotions as if they were their own. Quaid lowered himself to one knee and his army followed suit, thousands of tiny humans paying what respect they could to the sacrifice of an unfathomable being.

Coynera cried once more.

Dragon Dream
Kerstin Schulz

Out of a kernel-core
grew a broadening
paper thin shell –
a slick-sticky rustling
unfolded –
a body iridescent
as a damsel fly's wing –
lighter-than-air
bourn upward –
awkward body
wing-guided
over ley-lines
of electrical wire –
I coughed
a wet-wood trickle of smoke –
not enough fire in my belly
to spark a candle flame –
then down I came
wind-weary dragon-wright
I refolded myself
into the white-robed
origami-woman
breathless
from her novice flight

"Dragon Tapestry" by Richard E Schell

Stage Magic
Karen Eisenbrey

Crett waited backstage for his cue. He wiped his sweaty hands on his shirt and tried to calm his breathing, sucking in lungsful of warm, rose-scented air. He tied his curly red hair back to keep it out of his face. Crett had never been so nervous, and that was saying a lot. It didn't help that the play was being performed outdoors. He preferred seeing plays inside the theater. For as long as he could remember, Crett had been prey to disabling fear, especially of open spaces. After years working through the reasons for his fear, he was less jittery about being outside than in the past, though it would never be his favorite. But Crett had to accept that his part in this show was best performed outdoors.

Performed. There was another reason to be nervous. Crett had no desire to be onstage in front of an audience. He was more than happy to leave the acting, singing, and dancing to his friends Jumi and Frizza, twin siblings he'd known since early childhood. Both had been members of this theater troupe for a couple of years, putting on shows in the city and traveling to smaller towns like old hands. Most of Crett's responsibilities in this show were behind the scenes, but he had a big, public part to play at the end. If it worked.

"Are you ready?" Frizza emerged from the troupe's wagon with the rest of the small cast, costumed for her role as a Townsperson.

"Yes. I think," Crett muttered. "I hope."

"You'll be great." Jumi, in a wizard's cloak and false beard, slapped Crett on the back. "I can't wait to see it."

"Thanks." Crett smiled weakly and concentrated on not vomiting.

The players gathered in the wings as a small band played the opening music. Against his better judgment, Crett peeked around the backdrop at the audience. Nearly every seat was filled, with his family in the middle of the front row and his mentor, Wizard Larem, one row back with Wizard Terulo. Crett's parents weren't looking his way, but his older sister waved at him and Grandma Stell smiled proudly. Crett ducked back out of sight, fighting panic. He was glad his family was there. Grandma had traveled all the way from Deep River for this show. It wasn't her first trip to Eukard City, but her visits were rare enough that her presence stood out. She and the rest of them would support him even if he failed. But in the rows behind them ... *wizards*! And not just Larem and Terulo. All of them.

Crett wasn't supposed to be in the theater. Since the age of thirteen, Crett had been studying magic. It had come to him late and with difficulty, but it was the family business. His father was a powerful wizard, well regarded in the community. Crett's grandfather had been a wizard, too; a difficult character by all reports, but with dramatic flair. Crett's mother was a skilled magical healer. His sister was one of only a few women to attain the title of wizard. They had all been pleased and proud when Crett finally discovered his own magic.

There wasn't much choice about whether to train that power. Untrained magic was dangerous. After some introductory lessons with his family, Crett had enrolled at the Wizards' Hall, completing his formal education in the spring, just after his seventeenth birthday. All that remained was today's demonstration of what he'd learned on his own—the completion of his quest.

When Crett began his quest four months before, he'd had no assurance it would get even this far. He would never forget that first meeting about it with his mentor.

Four months ago

Crett and Wizard Larem sat at a table in one of the smaller workrooms upstairs at the Wizards' Hall, a grand old mansion converted long ago into a social center for the wizards of Eukard City. In the past, aspiring wizards would have found mentors there, apprenticing with one instructor who would train them until they were ready for the final quest. The magic school had been formalized within Crett's lifetime; he didn't remember exactly when. Rather than learning from only one teacher, beginning students learned elementary magic from an array of wizards—whoever was most expert in an area of study. Crett enjoyed learning from almost everyone, including his sister and father. Wizard Larem was the one exception, so Crett was shocked to be assigned to him as apprentice when it was time to learn more advanced magic. But he must have learned enough—he had just passed a long examination, answering questions about theory and demonstrating his skill with illusions, moving and manipulating objects, setting and extinguishing fires, speaking mind-to-mind, and transformation. He became a crow and hopped across the table before resuming his own form.

"I will never understand why anyone would wish to take other forms," Wizard Larem muttered. He wore his usual expression, as if he had just stepped in dung. His almost colorless hair hung to his shoulders. A patchy beard adorned his chin. Perhaps he couldn't decide which he hated more, shaving or facial hair. Crett could hardly criticize. Razors unnerved him, too, though his beginner's beard rarely needed such attention. "But you did it skillfully. I would not have known you from a real crow."

"Thank you," Crett said, unsure whether he had been praised or insulted. A common experience with his mentor.

"I have been asking all the questions," Larem continued. "Do you have any questions for me?"

"Why did you accept me as apprentice?" Crett asked in a rush, before he could change his mind.

"I believe I was the only one with an opening at the time."

"All right, but you could have said no," Crett said. "I know you don't like me."

"*Didn't*," Larem corrected. "I don't like many people. They're so ... messy. And they smell bad."

"Sorry. I sweat when I'm nervous." *And I'm always nervous.*

"You're no worse than most, and better than many." Larem gazed past Crett. "Do I frighten you?"

"Everything frightens me," Crett said.

Larem smiled. "Perhaps in the past."

Crett was sure this rare smile from his mentor was meant to put him at ease, but he found Larem's grimace more disturbing than the look of perpetual disgust.

"I have watched you overcome many of your fears," Larem continued, unaware of the effect his expression had on his apprentice.

"Is it really *overcoming* if you have to do the thing while you're still afraid of it?"

"Young man, that is the definition of courage."

Crett's face warmed under this near praise. He hoped his dark skin would hide the flush from Larem, who disapproved of physical responses.

"I wasn't sure you had any courage when we began," Larem continued. "And yet, here we are, ready to discuss your wizard's quest. What will you do?"

"I have an idea," Crett said. "I don't know if it's any good. My friends and I wrote a play—they're in a theater troupe now, but when we were children, we put on lots of skits. They did most of the acting and I helped with backdrops and things. This is their first full-length play."

"An amusing project, I'm sure, but this does not sound like a quest," Larem said. "You are supposed to design an experience in which you learn unfamiliar magic on your own, without help from your mentor, and in your case, from your family."

"I'm getting to that," Crett said. "We chose 'The Quest for Dragon Scales' to turn into a play. Do you know that story? My grandmother tells it, and—"

"I am familiar with the tale. Proceed. How is this a quest?"

"The director accepted the script, as long as the dragon is impressive." Crett clenched his fists under the table to stop his hands' shaking. "I'm supposed to ... provide the dragon."

"So your play has the word *quest* in the title." Larem drummed his fingers on the table. "Puppets and costumes do not make a wizard's quest."

"I didn't say anything about puppets," Crett replied. "I mean, there might be puppets, but I plan to make an illusion of the dragon."

"Crett, I know you are already skilled with illusions."

"Not like this, though," Crett said. "I need to create a convincing illusion of something none of us has seen in real life. Take what the audience imagines when they hear a dragon story and put it in front of their eyes. I don't already know how to do that."

The way people imagined dragons, they were always big and powerful. Nothing like Crett. He was tall, but scrawny. Not intimidating at all. His sister was more intimidating than Crett was. Even his mother was, and she was tiny. Could he create a convincing dragon? That was the challenge that made it a quest.

"Hmm." Larem stroked his uneven little beard, then withdrew his hand and looked at it with disapproval. "Where will you begin?"

"The library?" Crett said. "I'm sure I've seen illustrations in some of the old books."

Larem nodded. "Terulo would know. And he's not related to you."

Crett's hopes soared. Wizard Terulo was like an uncle to Crett, but he was not kin. And before he was Eukard City's librarian, he had been Larem's apprentice.

"Do I have your approval, then?" Crett asked.

"Why not? Let me know when you're ready to give a demonstration."

Crett left the Wizards' Hall, exhausted from the examination and the intense conversation, but elated that his quest idea had gained Larem's approval. He was over the first hurdle. If he succeeded to his mentor's satisfaction, he would be finished with school and apprenticeship. He could chart his own course.

"You want *me* to advise you on your quest?" Terulo asked. "I'm honored. Flattered, even. But you know I don't have enough power to work spells."

"I don't need you to work spells," Crett replied. "I need you to help me find books."

"We haven't had a library quest in years," Terulo said. "Not since mine. What kind of books do you need?"

"Any with dragons in them."

"I'm going to need to hear the whole story," Terulo said. "Let's sit upstairs."

Crett followed the librarian up a spiral staircase to the mezzanine, where books related to magic were kept. Study desks sat under the tall windows, vacant on this spring afternoon. Terulo pulled two chairs up to the nearest and took a seat. Crett sat in the other and told the same story he had told Larem. Terulo let him talk without interruption, stroking his neat beard—at odds with his unruly dark hair—without any of Larem's self-consciousness.

"An unusual but worthy quest," Terulo said. "You're helping your friends with theirs at the same time." He went to the shelf of folk tales and pulled down three volumes. "These should get you started. These two are illustrated. This one isn't, but it has dramatic descriptions."

Crett opened the first of the illustrated books. It had block-printed images at the beginning of each tale. He quickly flipped past the depiction of Old Mother Bones, a towering, skeletal witch in tattered clothes. That character had given him too many nightmares over the years. He stopped when he came to "The Quest for Dragon Scales."

It was an exciting adventure tale about a wizard searching for a dragon to obtain three of its scales—needed ingredients for a magical ritual to break a curse on the wizard's village. This version ended differently than the one Crett's grandmother told, with the wizard slaying the uncooperative dragon with an enchanted sword. Crett preferred Grandma's version, in which the dragon is also under an enchantment, imprisoned on a bare mountaintop far from its own kind. The dragon begs the wizard to lift the curse in exchange for the scales. Although it could be a dangerous trick, in the end the wizard agrees to lift the spell. The dragon does not attack, but flies joyfully away, dropping the needed scales as it goes. Crett assumed this version was Grandma Stell's own invention. It was just like her to have everyone win in the end.

The illustrated dragon was a bulky creature, crouched on four thick limbs ending in clawed feet. It had three horns on its head and a doglike muzzle, open to show sharp teeth. After studying the picture, Crett produced a small illusion, about the size of a kitten, to get a better idea of the creature's shape.

"Would it be all black if it were real?" Terulo asked.

"No, that's just how it's printed in the book. The story describes red, blue, and green scales." Crett created a new illusion with color and made it move. "I don't know. This shape looks clumsy, and at full size, it might be too frightening."

"Isn't that the effect you want?"

"More ... amazement."

Crett let the illusion go and opened the other illustrated book. It had line drawings, more graceful than the block prints. He flipped through pages until he came to a dragon story—not the same tale, but he liked this image more. This dragon had a sinuous shape, with large wings, backswept horns, and a long, narrow snout. Crett created an illusion in this shape, red at the head and cooling to green and blue down the length of the body. It took several tries to make the body undulate and the wings flap believably.

"That's pretty," Terulo said. "Does it breathe fire? That would add drama."

"It does now." Crett added flames to the illusion. The tiny dragon coiled and uncoiled, flying around their heads, flapping its wings and breathing fire until Crett let the illusion go.

"How big does it need to be?"

"According to my friends' boss, big enough to make the actor playing the wizard look small," Crett said. "It should fill the stage and have scales large enough to be easily visible at the back of the audience."

Terulo stepped away to the other end of the mezzanine, a distance about the same as from the stage to the back of the theater. Crett created illusions of progressively larger scales until the librarian signaled that a palm-sized object registered as a dragon's scale. He returned to Crett's table.

"Will you need to create the scales by magic, or only the dragon?"

"The scales can be props, painted and spangled to really show up," Crett said. "Knowing how big they are will help me present a convincing dragon. I hope."

Crett returned to the library in the days that followed to continue studying the illustrations and descriptions of dragons. He practiced and refined his small illusion until it looked and moved like a real creature. The next challenge: enlarging the illusion to be convincing at what he imagined as life-size. To preserve the secrecy of the project, he practiced this part in his room at home, with the door shut. His family knew the basics of his quest, but he wasn't allowed to seek their advice. Easier on everyone if he kept it to himself.

He started by flying the small illusion around his room, controlling how high it flew and where it was looking. It required more attention to detail than any illusion he had tried before, more like working a complicated puppet than simply presenting an image. He allowed it to perch on the windowsill to simulate landing on the stage. The first few times, it hovered above the surface or sank into it. When Crett was confident the dragon looked like it had weight, he repeated the exercise with a dragon the height of a large dog, with a snaky body of proportional length. By the time it had flown around the room a few times and set its feet on the floor, Crett was trembling and sweating from the effort. Illusions were usually easy for him, but the larger size required more power. And he had never needed to keep one visible and in motion for this long.

Maybe he only needed more practice, but it worried him. The dragon needed to be much bigger. Crett continued to enlarge the illusion—the height of a deer, then of a bison, until it was twice as tall as any animal he'd seen. It filled his room, with no space to spread its wings. Within a short time, he was dizzy from expending power. The dragon grew transparent, then vanished as Crett collapsed onto his bed.

This was not going to work.

"That's why it's a quest," he reminded himself. "It's supposed to be a challenge."

Crett returned to the library for advice and sympathy.

"I can't sustain it for as long as it needs to be on stage," he told Terulo.

"There's no one else here right now," Terulo said. "Show me?"

Crett handed Terulo a copy of the script. "You read the wizard's part. I'll be the dragon. We start with it flying." Crett had the small version fly around a few times. "Then it lands on the stage and talks with the wizard." The little dragon landed on a desk, looking toward where the wizard character would be while Terulo read the wizard's lines. The dragon's mouth opened and closed when Crett spoke its lines. "Then it flies away." The dragon lifted off and flapped away before Crett let the illusion go.

"That was perfect!" Terulo exclaimed.

"In miniature, sure."

"Show it at full size. Is there enough space here?"

"More than in my bedroom," Crett said with a wry half-smile.

This time, the illusion dragon was nearly as long as the mezzanine, and taller than the bookshelves. Crett had it circle the inside of the library before landing. Terulo was only halfway through the wizard's speech when it began to flicker and fade.

Crett sat in a chair, breathing hard. "See? It can't just blink out in the middle of the scene."

"That would be a problem." Terulo walked up and down, considering the problem. "The small illusion would be perfect for showing the dragon flying in the distance. What if you did the big one another way?"

Crett nodded. "Like a puppet? It might not fulfill my quest, but it would work for the show, I guess."

"I wasn't thinking a puppet, though that could be part of it," Terulo said. "But you have another talent, something no one else does. Why not use that?"

Crett frowned. "I don't ..." Then he understood. He did have a unique talent, but he'd never found a use for it. "That will take a lot of power, too, but I wouldn't have to hold it for the whole scene. If I can do it at all."

"But if you can," Terulo said with a broad smile, "what a way to complete your quest!"

Crett spent the next few weeks working on his project—mostly in his mind. He couldn't work this magic in his small bedroom, or really, any indoor space. Doing it outdoors was a sure way to spoil the surprise. So he walked around for days on end with his head full of dragons.

In the middle of this process, his friends came to visit.

Frizza plopped onto his bed. "We need to show the boss something," she said. "She likes the script, but she won't schedule the show unless the dragon is worth seeing."

"Our first show with a real theater troupe!" Jumi exclaimed. He perched on the only chair, so Crett sat on the floor. "I know you won't let us down, Crett."

"Will she be satisfied with the miniature version?" Crett sent the small dragon flapping around his room. Frizza and Jumi had seen it before, so that wouldn't spoil anything.

"Impressive, for its size," Jumi said. "Can you make it big?"

"I think so." Crett beckoned them closer so he could whisper his plan.

Frizza's eyes widened. "You can do that? Let's go see her right now!" She was out the door before Crett could reply.

They met the director at the theater. She was a tall woman, almost eye-to-eye with Crett, her silver-streaked black hair pulled back in an untidy knot.

"Your friends tell me you can give us an impressive dragon."

Crett cleared his throat and produced the miniature dragon. It flapped around the theater, then swooped down to alight on the director's shoulder. Crett had it look directly at her before letting the illusion go.

"It's not very big," the director said.

"No, that's for when it first appears in the distance," Crett explained. "We can do big puppets for when it meets the wizard."

"And for the finale, when the dragon flies away?"

"I'm working on something … dramatic. It wouldn't be a good idea to try it indoors."

The director nodded slowly. "If it's anything like your small sample, I'm inclined to say yes. And to take this show on the road afterward."

Crett's belly fizzed with nerves. He'd never considered going on the road with the troupe. But he would have his friends with him. They were in this together.

"Trust us, it'll be amazing," Frizza said.

Who was she reassuring, and how could she be so certain? But if it worked, it *would* be amazing. And if it didn't? An utter failure, and not only for Crett.

The Play

Crett let the distant splashing of the fountain soothe his nerves and focused on thoughts of Grandma Stell as the performance began. The townsfolk met with their wizard about the curse on the village, then sent him away on his quest for the dragon's scales. Crett listened closely to their disembodied voices.

His first cue! Crett created the small illusion dragon to fly a few passes above the backdrop. He enjoyed the appreciative gasp from the audience. He let the illusion go, then turned a crank as the dragon made a closer appearance in the form of a colorful puppet. It undulated and flapped its wings, thanks to a series of cranks and cams—the same mechanism that transformed wooden cutouts into ocean waves in other shows. For the meeting with the wizard, Crett joined another stagehand to work a large puppet of just the dragon's head, three times taller and broader than Jumi in his wizard garb. Crett couldn't see anything that was happening, but the audience's reactions told him they were enjoying the production. The story and the puppets, at least, were a success.

While the wizard worked the spell to free the dragon, Crett left his fellow stagehand to manage the dragon puppet as it withdrew. It was time to play his biggest part. He closed his eyes and reached inside himself to find the dragon's heart. He had thought about it, studied it. In his mind, he had *been* it. He knew the dragon almost as well as he knew himself.

With a few whispered words, Crett transformed from a gangly human boy to a sinuous, scaled creature of red, blue, and green. He flapped enormous wings and leaped into the air above the stage. The audience shrieked as he soared over them, toothy jaws open wide. Wizard Larem gaped. Jumi triumphantly displayed three glittering scales. The audience cheered.

Crett soared to a safe height and breathed a stream of fire. Not an illusion—real flame. The audience cheered. He circled overhead a few times, reluctant to give up this powerful form. But ... he had his own power. Some wizards could take other forms, but no one transformed into imaginary creatures. No one but Crett. He landed heavily on the stage and returned to his gangly self. If anything, the audience cheered louder. For once, Crett didn't mind the attention, though his hair had come undone and flopped into his face. He bowed, grinning at Grandma Stell in the front row. He caught his mentor's eye where he sat among the wizards. Larem nodded approval and slowly clapped his hands.

Crett had completed his quest. He was no longer an apprentice. Whether he could grow a beard or not, he was a wizard, like his father and sister. But his own kind of wizard, with his own kind of magic.

A theater wizard. Which story would he tell next?

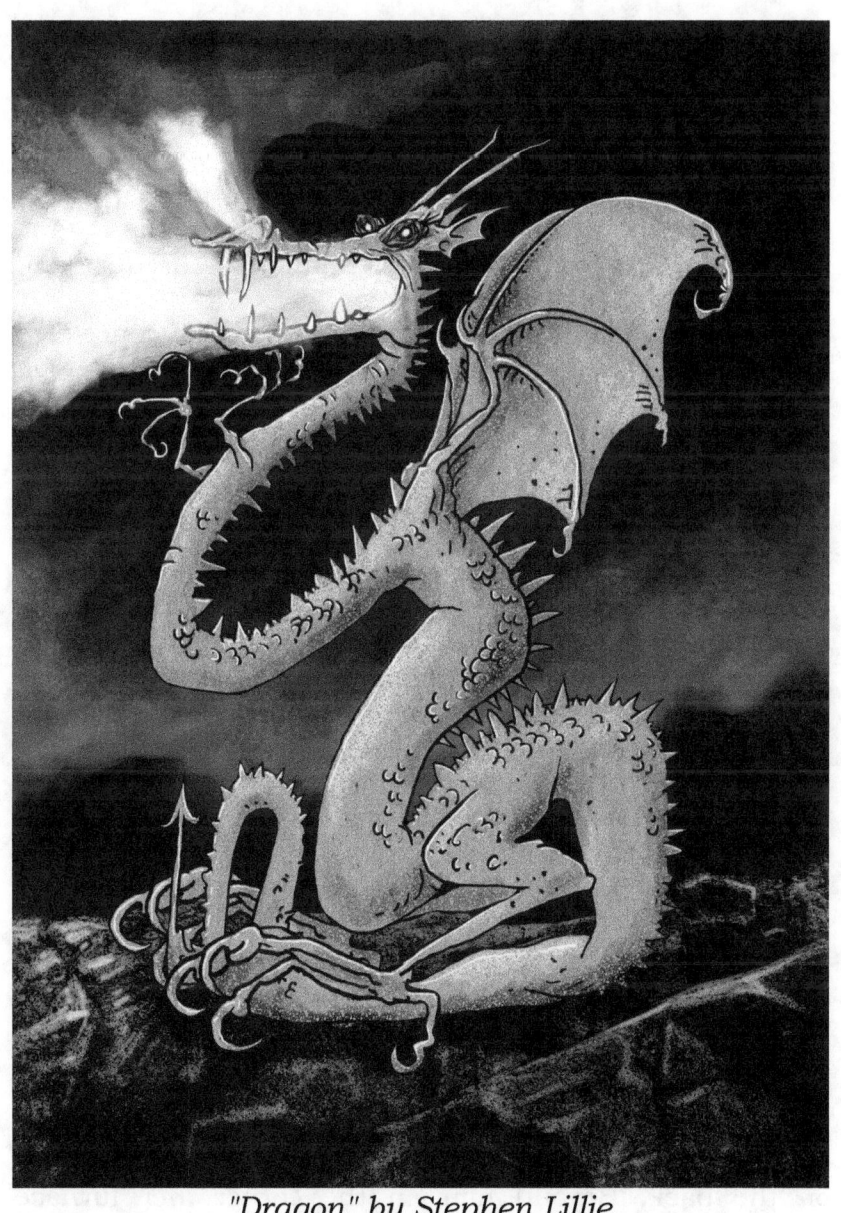
"Dragon" by Stephen Lillie

Gladys Tuttle and the Iguana Incident
David Hankins

Gladys sat in her kitchen, tapped a gnarled finger on her teacup, and stewed. Three days since the Iguana Incident. Three days of recriminations, threats, and lawyers. All aimed at her.

Then, as if fate were having a lark, her furnace died during Bozeman's worst arctic front in decades. On Christmas eve. Sub-zero temperatures clouded her windows with feathery frost. Icy winds howled as the repairman banged around in the basement.

Merry freaking Christmas.

Gladys glared at her tea, feeling adrift. She'd always had a driving purpose. Raise her kids, be a supportive wife, work hard for that next promotion. Well, the kids were grown, she was a fifty-nine-year-old divorcée, and Mayor Braun himself had fired her on Saturday.

Gladys brushed short gray hair behind one ear and sipped her tea. *Calming Mint*, the bag read. She harrumphed. Stupid tea was defective. She didn't feel calm, but at least it warmed her hands.

A tremendous crash and a blood-curdling scream rocketed Gladys to her feet. She sprinted for the basement stairs.

Well, hobbled with purpose. Blasted wonky knee.

Her musty basement was a collapsed wreck of shelves and boxes. Brandon the repairman stood in the center of the chaos, his back turned. He was a broad, bearded man who looked like a lumberjack, but with more fat than muscle, and wore one of those ridiculous holiday sweaters that had Rudolph's face on the front and his rear on the back. Beyond him, in the corner, her furnace looked like a beast had shredded it.

From the inside.

Brandon shoved something red and writhing into Gladys's old cat carrier.

"What is *that?*" she demanded, finger thrust at the rattling cat carrier.

Brandon's head whipped around, eyes wide. "Raccoon."

"With red scales?"

"I meant iguana."

"Liar! I work ... worked in animal control. That is *not* an iguana." She would know. Gladys snatched the carrier and glared inside. Her breath caught.

A hatchling dragon hissed at her and flared bat-like wings, filling the cramped space. It was almost two feet long, with a thin, snake-like body and an arching neck.

Her jaded heart fluttered and the scowl on her face melted just a bit. The little thing was adorable. Impossible. A creature from fairy tales that shouldn't exist.

And yet.

"That's a dragon," Gladys said, brows furrowed but unwilling to sound anything less than confident.

"What? Nooooo. Dragons aren't real." Brandon smiled innocently behind that absurd beard.

Gladys eyed the furnace that Brandon had installed twelve years ago. Jagged sheet metal curved outward. "Why was there a dragon in my furnace?"

"Merry Christmas?" Brandon mimed the open-palmed gesture of giving her a present. He wilted under Gladys's scowl then sighed. He ran fingers through his thick hair. "Dragon eggs produce controllable radiant heat when properly wired. Cheap and reliable but they never hatch. I've used them for years!"

"Where does one acquire dragon eggs?"

"I've got a guy. Actually, I think he's a goblin, but—"

Gladys snorted. "Poppycock! Next, you'll have me believing in unicorns and elves."

"Says the lady holding a *dragon*." Brandon hunched his shoulders and shoved his hands in his pockets.

Gladys narrowed her eyes. Brandon's cell phone jangled. He answered and a woman's high-pitched scream erupted from the other end. Gladys didn't understand everything, but she heard enough.

Another egg had hatched.

Brandon gave assurances that he was coming, but his wild-eyed expression said he wanted to run for the hills.

Gladys arched an eyebrow when the call cut off. "How many dragon-egg furnaces have you installed?"

"Um, two hundred? Two fifty?"

"You fool." She raised the carrier and considered the hatchling. It scrabbled at the back, claws gouging thick curls of plastic. Gladys cooed and it froze, head cocked. It mimicked the sound, adding a little upward trill at the end. The little darling. She eyed Brandon. A sense of purpose filled her, something she hadn't felt in a long time.

"I'll help retrieve the dragons."

Brandon sagged with relief. "Thank—"

"But you *will* replace every furnace for free."

The idiot man gulped but nodded. She could see in his eyes that he'd expected worse. Perhaps that she'd call the cops and turn him in for fraud and endangerment.

He didn't know that Bozeman PD wouldn't take her call. Not after the Iguana Incident had leveled City Hall.

Gladys shook herself and headed for the stairs. "Come," she said. "We're going dragon hunting."

***

Crystallized snow whipped around Brandon's utility truck as they navigated Bozeman's narrow streets. The radio prophesied two more days of sub-zero temperatures with lows down to negative forty. Between them, the hatchling gnawed at the bars of its carrier.

Gladys drummed her fingers on a spare cat carrier on her lap and her lizard catchpole, lost in thought. She glanced at Brandon. "What made you try wiring eggs into a furnace?"

Brandon bit his lower lip, making his beard puff out. "It was actually Emyl's idea."

"Emyl?"

"My parts guy. The goblin. Nobody bought his 'authentic dragon eggs,' thinking it was a scam, so he tested different uses for them. Emyl demonstrated their heating capabilities, then sold me the whole lot for a bargain."

"A price too good to be true?"

"Uh, yeah. Sort of."

Gladys pursed her lips and eyed the neighborhood. She knew these streets. Her ex and his new wife lived right ... there. The Wentworths. Gladys had reclaimed her maiden name, Tuttle, to create distance after the divorce. It had been bad enough seeing James at work: her running animal control and him as Bozeman's Police Chief.

She grimaced when Brandon parked in front of a brick two-story whose windows and eaves were lined with Christmas lights. Of course the call had come from the Wentworths. Just her luck.

With a resigned sigh, Gladys grabbed her equipment and followed Brandon into the cold. It was a sharp cold. The kind that sent jagged icicles into your lungs.

Brandon knocked and a blonde bombshell answered. Well, mostly blonde. Gray hinted at Johanna Wentworth's roots. She wasn't quite as far past her prime as Gladys, but looked decades younger with flowing hair, lacquered nails, and an implanted hourglass figure that must have cost a fortune. Gladys felt short and frumpy in comparison.

"Where have you been?" Johanna yelled. "That creature ..." Her eyes bulged when she recognized Gladys. "You can't be here. We got a restraining order this morning!"

On Christmas Eve? Small surprise nobody had bothered to inform Gladys. She scowled and brandished the catchpole. "Do you need animal control or not?"

"You blew up Jimmy's office. We're supposed to be in Tahiti celebrating our third anniversary, but we had to cancel because of *you*!"

Had it really been three years since James married his latest fling? Gladys should have left them alone, but his betrayals still hurt despite the years.

Brandon turned, eyebrows raised. "The City Hall explosion ... that was you?"

"It wasn't my fault." At least, she didn't think it was.

Johanna crossed her arms, pushing her implants upward. "Tell it to our lawyer. Jimmy's with him now."

"I tried. Now, will you let us in, or have you decided that you like your new pet?"

Johanna's glare could have melted the thin snow on the porch, but she stepped aside.

Gladys barged inside, ignoring Brandon's curious stare.

They found the hatchling dragon upstairs in Johanna's walk-in closet, sprawled amidst ruined ball gowns lined in genuine gold. Who went to balls in Montana? Pretentious twit. The dragon rolled around like a cat on catnip and gnawed on a sequined bra.

Gladys knelt and extended her catchpole.

"Hey, little one," she said softly then cooed and clucked her tongue. The dragon dropped its mouthful of bra and cooed back with the same upward trill the first dragon had used. Gladys mimicked the sound, slipped the catchpole's leather loop around its neck, and cinched it tight.

The dragon went nuts.

Razor-sharp claws tore at the aluminum pole. Fire burst from the hatchling's maw. A line of hanging sweaters flared up as the creature writhed and scrambled.

Gladys fell back, struggling with the pole. "Brandon! The carrier!"

The repairman lunged forward, but before he could secure the dragon, the pole snapped under its claws.

The dragon landed, singed the carpet with more fire, and scrambled for the hall. Johanna's scream echoed from downstairs, warbling as she ran. The front door opened and slammed, shaking the old house.

Gladys pulled herself upright and knocked the burning clothes to the floor with her pole. She stomped the fire out, leaving a smoking mess that smelled like burned plastic. Even Johanna's clothes weren't real.

Pounding footsteps preceded Johanna, who yelled at Brandon. "I got rid of that iguana, no thanks to you! Sent it out the front door."

Gladys harrumphed. "It's not an iguana."

Johanna whirled toward the closet. Her jaw dropped. "What have you done?"

Gladys raised warding hands. "This isn't what it looks like."

"You burned my clothes!"

"No, the dragon—"

"Dragons aren't real."

Brandon raised a finger. "That's what I said!"

Gladys glared at them both. Johanna pulled her phone from her back pocket and dialed.

"This is Johanna Wentworth, the chief's wife. I'm reporting an arson."

Gladys's jaw clenched. This wasn't her fault! It was the Iguana Incident all over again. Nobody would believe her. They never did.

She grabbed the empty cat carrier and Brandon's sleeve then stomped downstairs and out the front door. No sign of the little dragon. Gusting winds had whipped the thin snow over any tracks.

Brandon shrieked and bolted for his truck. The passenger window was a slagged wreck, melted glass reformed into frozen streams down the door. He yanked the door open, revealing an empty, half-melted cat carrier.

Great. They'd lost both dragons.

Gladys pushed past Brandon, climbed in, and slammed the door. Johanna appeared on the porch, yelling into her phone, "She's getting away!" Gladys rolled her eyes.

Brandon stood in the blowing snow, looking lost. "Now what?"

"We need help." She didn't want to call Sal, her former deputy who'd supported her sacking—and been promoted afterwards—but dragon hunting clearly required more robust equipment.

Good heavens. Dragons. Sal would laugh in her face!

Brandon nodded. "Agreed. Let's go see Emyl."

Hmmm. Asking a goblin for help sounded much better than facing Sal. Gladys cocked one eyebrow. "Well, what are you waiting for? The police?"

A siren sounded in the distance.

Brandon moved surprisingly fast for such a large man.

***

Gladys huddled into her heavy down jacket as they drove, sub-zero winds whipping through the melted window.

"So," Brandon said. "You blew up City Hall."

"They haven't proved that."

"What happened?"

Gladys spread her fingers over the heating vent, trying to capture some warmth. "It was supposed to be a prank. A bit of petty revenge for my ex." She'd ignored James's wandering eye for years before the divorce, but resentment had made her reckless. Foolish. "Someone abandoned a five-foot-long iguana in Lindley Park on Friday, and I rescued it. With James and Johanna supposedly out of town this week, I saw the opportunity for a little revenge."

Brandon grinned. "You put the iguana in his office."

Gladys blew on her fingers and nodded. "With food and water to last a week, and the radiator turned up high so he'd be comfortable. Iguana Don—that's what I named him—would have wreaked havoc while James was gone. Have you ever smelled iguana crap?" She shuddered.

"What went wrong?"

"I don't know. The building exploded an hour after I left." Poor Iguana Don. "City Hall was closed on Saturday, so only the lizard died, but they caught me on video bringing him in. The lawyers dubbed it 'The Iguana Incident.' They're trying to find the connection between iguanas and explosions."

Brandon chuckled and pulled into a gravel lot on the northeastern edge of Bozeman, in the shadow of the Bridger Mountains. Emyl's Parts Emporium was a decrepit cement-block building decorated with tattered signs announcing the lowest prices in town. Open Every Day!

The door chimed when they entered and Gladys wrinkled her nose at the dense smell of old grease and stale sweat. At least it was warm. Brandon marched them toward the back past aisles of refurbished appliance parts. An old TV over the unattended counter greeted them with the local news. Brandon slapped the counter.

"Emyl, where are you, you lying prick?"

An old man with liver spots and greased back hair popped his head out of a doorway. Emyl was small with sagging skin, overlarge ears, and a unibrow that looked like a prehistoric caterpillar. He wore a heavy winter coat that hid his figure and when he smiled, his teeth appeared a little too sharp. Perhaps he really *was* a goblin.

"Brandon, buddy. What's wrong?"

"The dragon eggs. They're hatching!"

Emyl made shushing motions and eyed Gladys sideways. "Your, uh, heating elements are malfunctioning?"

"Can the act, Emyl. Gladys knows." Brandon gave the shopkeeper a brief summary of events. "So, why'd they hatch?"

Emyl drummed claw-like fingernails on the countertop. "I may have miscalculated."

Gladys crossed her arms. "How so?"

"Dragon eggs incubate for centuries. That's why dragons are so rare as to seem mythological."

"Where'd you find the eggs?"

Emyl waved vaguely at the Bridger Mountains looming outside. "In a cave. Snagged 'em right out from under the hibernating mother."

"Wait," Gladys said. "There's a dragon living outside Bozeman?" She shuddered. Life had seemed safer this morning. Simpler, before she'd believed in dragons and goblins.

Emyl grinned and wriggled his caterpillar unibrow. "Don't worry your pretty little head. She's not waking up anytime soon."

Gladys cocked an eyebrow. Pretty? She hadn't been pretty in decades. Old, cranky, and gnarled like an oak, but not pretty. "So, what was the miscalculation?"

Emyl's smile faded. "My guess? Constant electrical current worked like an incubator. This arctic snap made everyone crank their heat up and accelerated the process."

Brandon spluttered. "But ... you said they'd last for centuries!"

Emyl resumed his snake-charmer's smile. "And you proved me wrong. Congratulations! You've returned dragons to the world."

Brandon didn't look pleased with his achievement. "How do we stop them hatching?"

"You don't. Nature and magic are in control now."

Brandon scrubbed his face with both hands. "We need help catching them."

Emyl's hands and unibrow shot up. "No way. You bought 'em. This is your problem."

Gladys slapped the counter and Emyl jumped. "Think again, goblin."

Emyl's face went blank. "Goblin? I'm just an honest shopkeeper who—"

"Malarkey. But I don't care if you're human, goblin, or the damned tooth fairy. You created this problem; you're going to fix it. Or I'll make it my mission to expose you." Gladys glanced around the shop. "I wonder how much of this crap was reported stolen?"

Emyl raised his hands. "All right, no need to get nasty. I may have something that'll help." He slid into the back room and soon returned with a small wooden crate. Emyl set the box reverently on the counter. He flipped up a heavy lid lined with lead and retrieved an eight-inch golden egg.

Gladys's breath caught. "Is that a dragon egg?"

Brandon shook his head, eyes wide. "Right size, wrong color."

Emyl eyed them. "Nothing's hatching out of this. It's pure gold."

Gladys glanced around. "Odd thing to have in a used parts shop."

"It was a recent ... acquisition. From a special customer whose wallet was suddenly light when it came time to pay."

"And this helps us ... how?"

"Dragons are geovores who dig tunnels to follow veins of ore. They can smell it. Copper, tin, whatever. Gold is like catnip. Get this close enough and they won't leave your side."

The TV interrupted with the blare of an emergency broadcast. All heads pivoted toward the grim-faced anchor on the screen.

"We bring you an emergency announcement from Mayor Braun." The screen shifted to a heavily bundled Mayor Braun outside the ruins of City Hall. James glowered in the background in his Police Chief uniform, arms crossed.

"After an unprecedented series of explosions and fires across Bozeman," Mayor Braun said, "I have ordered the natural gas lines closed and purged, cutting off heat to over half the residents of our fair city. It was a difficult decision to make on Christmas Eve, especially in arctic conditions, but for the safety of ..." He droned on and Gladys turned to Emyl.

"Dragons eat metal? Like the copper pipes used for natural gas?"

He nodded, gaze focused on the TV.

"So, these explosions are the dragons' fault?"

"Maybe."

"Brandon," she said. "Did City Hall have one of your dragon-egg furnaces?"

He shoved his hands into his pockets and wouldn't meet her eye. "They, uh, had two. It was a big building."

Relief welled up in Gladys's chest. She *hadn't* blown up City Hall with the Iguana Incident. It was just bad timing. Those poor dragons must have hatched, started eating copper gas lines, then died when the building collapsed in the explosion.

A *whump* rattled the storefront windows, making everyone jump. Past overburdened shelves and faded window signs, Gladys saw flames billowing from Brandon's truck.

"No!" Brandon yelled and bolted for the door, Gladys and Emyl close behind.

The truck's crumpled hood lay twenty yards away. Acrid black smoke and golden flames roiled around two small dragons who gnawed on the engine block, melting steel with their fire before lapping it up. The end of Gladys's catchpole still dangled from one's neck.

"My truck!" Brandon cried.

Emyl grunted. "Huh. They must have crawled under the hood for the heat."

Gladys nodded. Animals do that in winter. She snatched the golden egg from the goblin and knelt. She almost dropped it—gold is heavy—but cooed at the dragons with the upward trill they'd used earlier. Both dragons perked up, trilled back, then stalked out of the flames. She called again, putting a note of command in her tone.

The dragons scurried forward, heads low, wingtips and tails dragging lines in the snow. Gladys suppressed a smile. She'd found a dragon call that sounded like an alpha. Both dragons sniffed the golden egg tentatively. She lowered it a bit more and they went at it like deer at a salt lick.

Gladys' knees popped as she rose, and the dragons wound about her feet with happy growls. "We're rescuing the hatched dragons," she said. "All of them. Here's the plan: Brandon, plot a route that will take us past everywhere you've installed dragon-egg furnaces. Make a loop that ends near Lindley Park downtown. You'll be driving that beast there." She pointed to a low-sided flatbed truck at the edge of Emyl's parking lot. It was stacked high with reclaimed copper pipes. "Emyl"—she turned to the goblin—"I assume you're coming."

"That egg's not leaving my sight," he said, focused on his treasure. Where *had* he acquired a golden egg?

"Good. You gather supplies. We'll need blankets, a megaphone, and coffee if you have it. You and I are riding in the back."

The goblin's penetrating gaze shifted to her face. "Of course I have coffee, I'm not a savage. What will you be doing, my dear?"

Gladys drew a deep breath of sharp air, then blew it out in a frozen cloud. "I'm calling the only person I know who can help us contain all these dragons."

Emyl nodded, snatched the golden egg back, and headed inside with Brandon. Gladys leaned down to run a hand over a dragon's scaled back as it rubbed against her. She really wasn't looking forward to this call. She pulled out her phone and dialed.

James answered with a yell. "You tried to burn down my house!"

Her jaw clenched. "It was a misunderstanding."

"Like blowing up City Hall? You're a menace!"

"That wasn't my fault, and I can prove it. But that's not why I'm calling. I need your help."

"You need help, alright."

"Stop being snarky and listen! Bozeman has an incursion of dragons who are causing the fires and explosions. I can lure them to Lindley Park, but we need the police to clear traffic, evacuate the park, and bring in Forestry's Predator Containment team."

James snorted. "Dragons. We're in the middle of a crisis and you want me to drop everything for a fairy tale? You're delusional!"

Gladys gripped the phone, wanting to scream. She needed his help or their chances of saving more than a few dragons dropped to zero. Her shoulders sagged. "Do this and ... I'll confess to the Iguana Incident."

There was a moment of silence. "Deal. I'm recording, go ahead."

Second thoughts made Gladys pause. Could she trust him? The man who'd lied for years about his affairs?

No, she couldn't. But James always had to win. He'd bring everyone together just to show them that she was crazy.

Gladys gave her confession, a version of the truth. Instead of simply leaving Iguana Don in James's office, she said she'd gained access through the utility room just below and had accidentally damaged a gas line while cutting through his floor.

"Got it," James said, sounding smug. "I'll have everything set up within an hour. Where should I send your police escort?"

Gladys told him, feeling sick but relieved. "Bring the fire department to Lindley Park, too. Just in case the dragons get difficult."

"Sure, why not?" She could almost hear James rolling his eyes. "Dragons. You really have lost it, Gladys. It'll be fun watching you make a fool of yourself."

Had he always been this cruel or had James changed as their marriage soured? Did it matter? He hung up, and Gladys' shiver had nothing to do with the cold.

***

Twenty minutes later, they rumbled out of Emyl's gravel lot and headed into town, escorted by a patrol car with lights, sirens, and two surly officers.

The officers had arrived skeptical. When they saw the dragons, skepticism almost turned to violence.

"Fire-breathing bats should be shot on sight," one had said.

Gladys had barely convinced them to stand down.

Now she and Emyl huddled under a pile of blankets against the truck's cab, arctic winds whipping around them as Brandon drove through town. The blankets kept her warm, but Gladys could feel the snot freezing in her nose.

She took a swig of black coffee from a travel thermos. Bitterness bit her tongue as warmth spread through her chest. God, she needed that! Emyl saluted with his own mug, eyes barely visible under a thick beanie that covered his ears.

They drove for two hours, collecting dragons. Gladys made dragon calls through the megaphone whenever Brandon stopped and the little darlings flowed out of houses and businesses. As Emyl had predicted, the dragons flew straight to the golden egg for a taste before they happily explored the buffet of copper pipes on the truck's bed.

The sun was setting by the time they turned onto Main Street and headed for Lindley Park. The flatbed was a writhing mass of feasting red dragons. Flames flickered as they melted pipes and ate.

Hatchlings crawled over Gladys and Emyl. The goblin practically buried himself under the blankets to avoid their prodding claws. He clutched the golden egg protectively, only bringing it out when a prodding nose grew too insistent. The dragon would lick it, give a shiver of pleasure, then rejoin its siblings at the copper buffet.

Police cars lined Main Street, blocking traffic. Flashing lights added a sparkle to the oversized Christmas decorations strung between downtown Bozeman's low buildings. Brandon turned into Lindley Park and the city fell away behind them. Brick buildings and gaudy displays gave way to ice-coated trees and snow-covered picnic tables.

The truck rocked to a stop amidst a collection of utility vehicles and a crowd of emergency personnel. Fire trucks, animal control, and—Gladys breathed a sigh of relief—Forestry's Predator Containment Team with its grizzly-bear-resistant cages. A clutch of reporters to one side began snapping pictures.

Brandon jumped out, shoulders hunched at all of the official attention. He tried slipping away but barely made it ten steps before an officer intercepted him.

Gladys stood, joints protesting painfully. A hatchling clung determinedly to her shoulder. James pushed through the crowd looking properly shocked for once.

"My God. Those really *are* dragons. How ...?"

"You wouldn't believe me. You never do." Gladys lifted the dragon from her shoulder and handed it to a woman from Forestry wearing heavy leather gloves. More folks stepped forward to help, but then a deafening roar shook the park.

Everybody froze. All eyes turned skyward.

Thirty feet of furious red dragon landed with a crash behind the truck, scales glittering in the flashing emergency lights.

The dragon mother! Gladys's knees buckled from the sheer magnificence of the beast. Deeply intelligent eyes focused on Gladys.

Hatchlings screeched happily, officers drew their sidearms, and the dragon roared again. The vibration shook Gladys to her core, but she whipped up the megaphone and yelled, "Don't shoot!" Nobody fired, but the weapons didn't lower either. Emyl burrowed deeper into the blankets.

The dragon mother stalked forward like an oversized bat, forelegs climbing onto the back of the truck. Shocks groaned and Gladys stumbled, but kept herself upright. The dragon eyed her like a snake watching a mouse.

Gladys had faced dangerous animals before. It came with the job. But never had she felt so confident that she was about to be eaten. Her mind blanked, screaming at locked-up joints to *run*.

She couldn't escape. She was old and slow. Her eyes darted to James and his officers. Fear painted their faces. White knuckles gripped their pistols. One wrong twitch from the dragon and they would kill it.

And the hatchlings.

Oh, hell no! Cold fury shot through Gladys, stiffening her spine. She would *not* be the cause of an entire species going extinct the same day it was discovered. There was only one thing to do. Convince the dragon that she was a friend.

Gladys lowered her eyes and gave the cooing dragon call. Her voice cracked a bit. She raised the little trill at the end, just like the hatchlings did, but without any note of command. She was not the alpha here. The dragon's head reared up, cocked to the side. It blinked double eyelids. Gladys cooed again and bowed her head. The hatchlings echoed her call and rose from the truck like a flock of starlings. They susurrated around the park before settling in the ice-coated trees.

She remained bowed, despite a sharp twinge in her back. The mother dragon stretched her neck forward and sniffed. The dragon smelled of damp earth and hot metal.

Heavens, those teeth were enormous.

The dragon sniffed again and growled.

"Emyl," Gladys said softly. "I need the gold."

"Hell no! It's mine." His voice was muffled under the blankets.

"Would you rather be a snack?"

There was a pouty silence before the blankets rustled and Emyl's gnarled hand popped out with the egg. The dragon's snout twitched toward it. Gladys retrieved the egg and presented it with another bow. A raspy tongue flicked out and the gold disappeared into the dragon's maw.

A rumbling sound like a purr vibrated the truck. Gladys cooed again, trilled upward, and the dragon responded. Deeper, more powerful, but happy.

Silence fell over the frozen park, broken only when the mother dragon leapt into the air.

The truck rocked from the assault and Gladys fell back onto Emyl. She watched the dragon and her hatchlings take to the sky. The red flock angled toward the Bridger Mountains and disappeared behind a ridge.

Gladys smiled. She had done it. The dragons were safe and heading home.

***

Gladys went to court for the Iguana Incident the following week, just after New Year's Day. With her confession, it was a slam-dunk prosecution. She tried to ignore James's smirk when the conviction was read. He always had to win.

Then came the sentencing. The judge eyed her over his wire-rim glasses. "Gladys Tuttle, in light of the uncommon courage and selflessness you displayed during the Dragon Incursion, and upon special request from Forestry, you are hereby sentenced to six months of community service."

Gladys blinked at him. "Excuse me?"

"Forestry wants your help dealing with this dangerous new species. Your first six months working for them will be without pay. You can negotiate terms of employment after that." He slammed his gavel, dismissed the court, and rose.

Gladys glanced at James whose triumphant smirk had soured. She shook her head. Forget him. She was done with that part of her life.

Time to move on.

A woman in a Forestry uniform stepped forward, hand extended. Gladys recognized her from Lindley Park. She'd taken the first hatchling.

"Ms. Tuttle? I'm Director Linwood. So glad to have you working with us. Is there anything you'll need before you start?"

Gladys shook the woman's hand, feeling a bit dazed, and nodded. "I need assistants who know about dragons. Emyl and Brandon have their hearing tomorrow. Perhaps you could recruit them as well?"

Brandon had sung like a canary when the cops started asking questions. Emyl had tried to slip away in the confusion but got caught trying to steal gear off the back of a firetruck.

Director Linwood smiled warmly. "I already spoke with the judge. He's leaning toward a hefty fine to cover damages in addition to community service. They should start with you on Monday. Welcome to the team, Dragon Wrangler."

Gladys smiled wryly. Nobody was wrangling that dragon mother with her intelligent eyes. But perhaps Gladys could create a safe haven, a space where humans and dragons could live in harmony.

"Thank you," she said and followed Director Linwood from the courtroom.

Ten days since the Iguana Incident, and Gladys had purpose once again.

Aging does not make women powerless objects of pity but colorful and entertaining individuals and, on occasion, fire-breathing dragons that wise people don't cross.

– Florence King

"At Night" by Angela Patera

Voyage of the Dragon Song
Anna Dallara

A smith wrought my head of spirit-silver on the prow —
I breathed life's fire into your ship,
Oars churned my blood,
My song filled the sails —
"Dragon Song," you named me,
"For the poets will sing our names forever."

The gods carved this land from a giant's corpse —
We sailed his tangled river-veins,
Gnawed his bones with axe and fang,
Prised gold from fortresses like clenched fists.
"Glory," you promised. "Valhalla."

You filled my belly with treasure,
Fought and bled on my deck,
Slept with your head on my planks —
We dreamed as one.

Years passed —
The Runes spelled our Fate,
Three Weavers wove you a shroud.
They buried us among the giant's bones,
Lying head to helm.

I wonder if you made it to Odin's great hall.
As for me, I guard your dust,
Try to recall the poets' words.
I sail alone in the dark.

Snowborn
Andrew Knighton

Uffeir Tuvasboon took the axes off the wall of his small, bare hut. The one-handed axe, which he'd chosen when he came of age, slipped through a hoop on his belt. His father's war axe he slung across his back before strapping on snowshoes of woven reeds and stomping out the door. It was a bright blue day, the sort that feinted with beams of sunlight before trapping you in freezing shadows. Uffeir wasn't falling for it. He kept his tunic buttoned tight even as sweat seeped from his skin, and squelched his way up the middle of the village, past low huts and their snorting, steaming pig pens.

"Ho, Uffeir!" Madde called as he passed her doorway. "Off to deal with the dragon?"

She said it like he was going to chop wood or gather lost goats, and Uffeir appreciated that. Staring fearfully at the sky and hiding behind shutters might keep the village quiet, but it didn't help fix the problem.

"Aye." Uffeir ducked his head, beard brushing the furs of his tunic. Madde sailed on the same raiding ships as Uffeir when Laird Lovar called for hands. She'd earned her scars and the gold that warriors scraped together fighting others' wars. She'd earned his acknowledgment.

"Come eat with me after." There was no guarantee of Uffeir having an "after", but Madde's smile was bright as southern days, her worries well buried. "I've a good haunch of goat and ale with it."

Uffeir knew what that invitation implied, but there was a reason he still lived in his father's small hut, a reason he'd chosen raiding over family life. He liked no company better than his own.

"Quit your scowling," Madde called at his back. "Life's too short to spend it cold and hungry."

Shrugging up his shoulders to block out her words, Uffeir marched on down the Silver Vale. Other villagers crept out to watch him go, people who had heard the dragon screeching in the night, who had found their goats torn to scarlet shreds on the snowy slopes. Frail elders, timid farmers, children too young to understand. All of them counting on him, the only beastbond for three vales east or west; a man who had tamed a Salt Cities gryphon and slain Marlesan mercenaries; a man who had fought with heroes and flown with monsters, or so the gossips said. Uffeir of the bloody axe and crooked nose.

Snow crunched beneath his feet, soft and pale as ashes after the raiders left. A southern wind carried the salt scent of the sea, and with it memories of straining at the oars, a hundred sailors fighting against a storm. If he'd been a man to smile, his lips might have curled.

An hour out of the village, just as the Silver Vale split in two, Uffeir caught the scent of the hot springs. Some said it turned their stomachs, but Uffeir had smelled the bodies in a city under summer siege, and this was no kind of rot. If anything, it was comforting, a smell he only found here. A smell of home.

With that smell came snorting and splashing. Creeping up the shallow left fork of the vale, Uffeir stopped at a bank of wind-blown snow, its surface melted by sunlight then frozen by shadows into a hard shell. He laid a hand on the axe by his side and peered over the snow.

The air above the springs shimmered from their heat. Steam hugged the banks, rolling around itself in the currents rising off the water. Fewer of the pools were exposed than had been at the start of the summer, those beneath the cliffs on the far side buried beneath ice and snow. Peeking from the water were the broken remains of old dragon eggs, thick as the planks of a ship, large enough that Uffeir himself could have curled up inside one of them. Bubbles from the steaming depths trickled up their sides and rippling water broke against jagged edges.

The dragon stood knee deep in the far end of the pool, its tail swishing from side to side through the water. It was an adult in its prime, as long as a raiding ship, its flanks covered in scales bright as diamonds. Vast muscles shifted as its long neck bent to sniff at the snow by the pool's edge.

Uffeir's heart swelled at the sight of the beast. In his years of fighting, he'd flown with two wyverns and a griffon, joining his mind to theirs each time, their spirits emboldening his while he calmed them enough to be ridden. But though he'd seen dragons over the vale since he was young, he'd never dealt with one up close. For the second time in a month, he nearly smiled.

Slow as ice drifting from the coast in spring, Uffeir crept out from behind the snowbank. He kept his axes strapped in place, arms free for balance. There had been a time when he didn't worry about falling, but there had also been a time when his hip didn't ache in a westerly wind.

Step by cautious step, he made his way around the edge of the pool. Everything would be easier if he could get to the dragon before it saw him. A hand against its flank, his mind sliding into its thoughts, the forging of a bond. He would coax the dragon away from the vale, perhaps take the chance to ride it before he triggered the instinct that would send it south, safely away from the village. It was too long since he'd flown with one of the great war beasts, pressed himself against its back and let it carry him aloft. He remembered the wind whipping his hair about, the reins tight in his hands, the warmth of a huge body against his and the slow thud of its heartbeat. Two hearts, two bodies, one purpose.

Strange that this beast hadn't flown south already. In Uffeir's lifetime, a score of dragons had laid their eggs in these pools, then left their mate to guard the egg while they flew south to feed and recover. The eggs hatched late in the summer, and the parents were gone with their newborns long before the first winds of winter. So why was this one here now, when snow bled from the soaring heights down to the empty fields?

The snow around the pool was treacherous, caught between the icy cold of the cliffs and the melting heat of the pools. A chunk slid away beneath Uffeir's foot and he flung his arms out to catch himself on a boulder.

Snow splashed into the water. The dragon turned.

Uffeir shoved off the rock and lunged towards the beast.

The dragon's head shot forward.

Uffeir leaped aside and teeth like daggers crashed where he had been. He rolled down a snowy slope, smacked his back on a rock, fell on his knees into a steaming pool. Fragments of one snowshoe littered the snow, and the other caught on an old shell as he rose.

Claws slashed and he tried to dodge again, but his foot was trapped and he fell sideways with a splash. Blood-warm water swallowed him and he gagged on the rot rushing into his mouth.

Claws tore through the murky water, fishing for Uffeir. He squirmed like a worm on a line and twisted in tight around his trapped foot. Pulling a knife from his belt, he sawed at the snowshoe's straps. He couldn't even drag in a breath to ease his aching chest, and the warmth in his head was more than the heat of the pool. At last, the leather gave way, and he shoved himself out, lungs burning. Claws churned the water as he burst out inside the dragon's reach, his war axe in his hands.

A less experienced warrior might have tried to fight the beast alone. He would have died. Uffeir blocked a blow that buckled both his arms and another that sent him stumbling. The third time, he let the dragon's claws carry the axe from his slippery hands, even as he stepped through and pressed a palm against its scaly hide.

Feelings rushed from the dragon into Uffeir. Longing. Frustration. Fear. The anguish of losing something more precious than words, made worse by the cruel hook of hope. A wave of anguish that threatened to drown his heart.

Uffeir forced himself to keep his hand against the scales, his mind pressed against the dragon's. He tried to show it safety and friendship, but those feelings were like fog parting before a raider's prow, so instead he pictured the villagers welcoming him home in the autumn, the warriors beside him in the battle line and on the oar benches, people he had come from and those he had gone to. And Madde, of course, with him in war and in peace.

Scales slid from beneath his fingers as the dragon stepped back. Uffeir sank shaking to his knees in the muddy shallows and waited for the claws to come for him. He had been too proud, thinking that he could tame a strange beast alone. He would pay with his life.

The dragon stared. A thought hung in Uffeir's mind, one solid vision amid the swirling emotions. A curved shell, mottled blue and green, lying in steaming waters.

An egg.

The dragon tilted its head towards the ice and snow that hid the edge of the pool. The mewling from the back of its throat almost broke Uffeir's leathery heart.

"Yours?" He made a cupping motion with his hands, then pointed at the snow. "Under there?"

The dragon made the plaintiff sound again.

Uffeir rose to his feet and faced the snow, water streaming from his beard and from the furs beneath his tunic. The pool was deeper here than by the other banks, its shallows buried beneath snow fallen off the mountainside. Water sloshed around his thighs as the dragon moved, and its warm breath made hairs stand up on the back of his neck.

A shiver shook Uffeir. Though the spring warmed his legs, an icy wind clawed at his face before snatching his frosted breath away. It would be worse under the snow. How would that affect a dragon's egg?

The beast leaned forward, its long neck brushing his shoulder. He'd never seen a dragon grieve before. What would it do when it gave up its child as lost? Lie down and die of a broken heart? Fly away from a valley made unbearable by bitter memories? Unleash its fury in a rampage against every living thing? He didn't know, and it didn't matter. What mattered lay under that deadly white drift.

The dragon pawed at the snow but more fell to take its place. A long, elegant head turned to look at Uffeir, pleading with him for answers. In Uffeir's experience, there was only one answer that ever mattered, and that answer was action.

He plunged into the snow, shoveling it aside with both hands. No point trying to clear it away, the snow was too thick and too soft for that. It would just keep falling to fill the gap. Instead, he wormed his body into the drift, finding his way by feel and downward instinct, letting the snow fall to fill the space where he had been. His flesh grew colder and he gritted his teeth to stop them rattling. Driven by an impulse that he wasn't even sure was his, he plunged into darkness and the bitter chill.

As he went deeper, his movements slowed with the cold and the weight of snow. Just a little further, he told himself, the egg couldn't be much deeper down, but even a little further became harder with each heartbeat, and those beats were slower than he liked.

Then his hand, straining stubbornly, touched something solid and smooth, something just warm enough to let him feel his fingers again. They felt like pain, but at least they were there. And though he couldn't see it in the dark beneath snow, he felt a mind within, faint as the wavering flame of a candle's last inch.

With muscles rigid from the cold, Uffeir twisted his body around, planted his feet on frozen dirt under the snow, wrapped his arms under the egg, and heaved. At first, it wouldn't move, but then the snow started to part. As slow as waking on the morning after a fight, he pushed it up, forcing the snow aside. Shivering with the strain as well as the cold, gritting his teeth around breaths spiked with ice, he forced the egg on. It started to move faster, the snow to part more easily. There was a roar like a storm wind and the egg was snatched away.

A patch of blue sky appeared through the pale drift. Uffeir scrambled up through the sudden opening, even as snow tumbled down to fill it. His numb arm gave way beneath him. He fell through and then down the outside of the snow bank, landed face first in the pool. The warmth was a wonderful pain, and for a moment he forgot that he was drowning. He pushed himself to his knees and spat out water that tasted like a long dead rat.

The egg lay in the steaming water, an exquisite curve mottled in green and blue, like the pillars he'd seen in the palace of a Salt City lord. Madde had mocked that place, with its grand arches and flimsy walls, but Uffeir had been glad of a season playing at guards after a year of proper war, and those pillars had been nice and cool to lean against in the summer heat. They'd reminded him of home, the first time he'd thought of returning with fondness rather than resentment. Funny how that had changed over time, how reluctant his footsteps had become the last time Laird Lovar came calling his warband.

The dragon crouched over the egg, so close that the small, thin scales of its cheek were almost pressed against the shell. It tapped the shell with the tip of a claw and something responded, but slowly and faintly. The dragon mewled, a soft sound rising into a high whine of distress. Its chest shook and so did the steep rock slopes around the pools. Snow thudded down on the far side and steam billowed and hissed as it hit the water.

Every youngster in the Vale came to see a hatching once, despite their parents' tales of a man who knew a man torn apart by a protective dragon. A young Uffeir and Madde had crouched high on the rocks above with two others close to them in age, had listened to the rapping of the infant's claws against the inside of its egg and the crack as it burst open, had pretended after that they weren't awed by what they had seen, because that was what the young did.

Thirty winters later, Uffeir was ready to embrace that awe, but the sound from inside the egg barely reached him from five strides away, never mind resounding sharply from the rocks above.

The dragon's wail became a broken, choking sound. Even before he placed a hand against its leg, Uffeir's eyes stung and his chest shook with an ache that went deeper than the cold.

There was another soft scratch, more feeble than the last, from inside the egg. The dragons laid their eggs in these springs for their warmth and this one had been buried beneath the cold instead. It was a wonder that any life remained. Uffeir knew that he should let it die, like any good farmer would the runt in a litter. But this was no mere piglet, no chick or calf. This was a dragon. It was majesty in flight, awe in battle, a cascade of bright scales shimmering in the sunlight. Amid the ice of winter or the ashes of war, it could fire him up with something more than grim determination. And as the parent dragon turned to look at him with wide eyes and parted lips, he knew that he couldn't abandon it.

The dragon made a sound as Uffeir approached the egg, half plea and half warning. In the steam from the pool, his fingers had thawed back from numbness through pain to a soft tingling. He ran them across the shell, feeling for any give, any weakness. But this was a dragon egg, thick as a ship's planks and twice as hard. Like the dome of that Salt City palace, its curve made it harder to break from outside than from within. Perfect protection; too perfect this time.

He took a deep breath, slid the axe from its hoop on his belt, and raised it. The dragon growled and bared its teeth. Uffeir swallowed, turned, stared into eyes like fire and teeth that could tear him in half.

"Let me do this or let your child die," he said.

The dragon wouldn't understand his words, but he hoped it would understand his meaning. If not, then he would end up like those goats shredded on the mountainside; not a dignified death, but he'd seen worse in war. He laughed at his own stupidity and wished that Madde was there to see him, so that he could become the story they used to warn youngsters away. Madde would know to make the story a funny one. This wasn't a hero's death, and he was cursed if he'd become some morbid tragedy.

The dragon's jaws opened wider. There was more scratching from the egg, fainter even than before. The creature hesitated, then turned away, hunching over to hide its face from what came next.

Uffeir let out a breath that hadn't ended up being his last. He raised the axe that he'd chosen when he came of age, summoned all the strength left in him, and swung.

The axe blade hit the egg with a sound like stone shot against city walls, then a click as a crack ran across the shell. Uffeir struck again, and this time a whole section fractured. He grabbed a piece with both hands, wrenched it out and flung it away. The film beneath burst, liquid dribbled down the marbled surface, and a snout emerged, with clawed feet to either side. A rough tongue snaked across the back of Uffeir's hand. He felt gratitude and relief, the joy of first touching the world, and wished it would linger there.

A crunch, a splash, and the baby dragon pulled itself out, wings tentatively unfurling, slender body slippery and eyes wide. With a rumbling purr and a breath that blew hot across the back of Uffeir's neck, the parent came to meet its young. Long necks coiled around each other and scaled cheeks pressed together. Their voices weren't exactly a song, but they weren't exactly not a song either.

Uffeir smiled from the depths of his soul.

***

It was almost dark by the time Uffeir trudged shivering back through the village. No one was out to see his return, not even a crack of light showing around well-made doors. But as he approached his home, huddled over and teeth chattering, wet feet numb from toe to heel, a door creaked open and warm light rolled out.

"Where are your axes?" Madde said as she threw him a blanket.

"Dropped them."

"Careless."

He tried to shrug, but his shoulders wouldn't join in. "I'll go back another day."

Most people would have asked him if he'd dealt with the dragon. Madde knew better.

"You want that warm meal now?" she asked.

Uffeir looked at his warrior's hut, a black block standing alone against the grey of twilight. Then he looked at Madde, smiling in the firelight that spilled out around her. His fingers touched the place where a rough tongue had run across the back of his hand.

"I suppose so," he said. "It's been a cold day."

Stained Glass Dragon
Katherine Quevedo

from the sharp webbing of its wings
slicing the air, to its bones like metal
frames for each radiant panel of flesh,

when it thrashes its long, prismatic tail
and pries its jaws, emitting molten
white-bright flashing tongues of light,

you see the heart, the source,
all the colors of afterimage
upon closed eyelids, but open now

to the spectacle of someone who
bends light to their will, who scalds
the air with their voice, an eternal roar,

for to witness a stained glass dragon
(and live) is to respect what refuses
to shatter, is to learn to roar with it

Slayer
Benjamin Spada

I.

I gave my team the *Cliffs Notes* version of the job and told them our helicopter was wheels up in thirty. For all they knew, it was a fairly standard mission. Standard by *our* measure at least. Loss of contact with a top-secret research facility, sensitive and dangerous project materials inside we couldn't chance getting into the wrong hands, a man in charge connected enough for our own boss, Mr. Rourke, to have a vested interest, and a need for *very* high caliber weapons. I'd deliberately withheld the finer details of the facility's research until our helicopter was a few thousand feet in the air. Figured that way, it'd be too late for my three teammates to abruptly bail out.

All things considered? They took it better than I expected.

"So... any questions?" I asked.

Our earmuffs let us hear each other clear as day without the deafening sound of the helicopter's rotors, but right now there was nothing but silence. To say that we could've heard a pin drop was a criminal understatement. Finally, it was our squad's designated marksman, Kelly, who stitched his face into a curious frown and broke the quiet.

"You mean like a... Komodo dragon?"

"No. A *dragon* dragon."

The squad's unofficial comedian, Billy, chimed in next. He smiled and looked all around the cabin as if he'd lost something.

"Okay," Billy said. "I've got one question: where you hiding him?"

"Who?"

"Ashton Kutcher. Come on out."

Kelly bit down on a knuckle to stifle a violent case of the giggles. Then, like a schoolboy, he raised his hand to ask another question.

"Cap, do we have any clarity on the size of the... uh... the *target*? The... hmm..."

"Just get it over with and say it, Kelly."

"Dragon. Yeah. The dragon. So, we talking Mushu from *Mulan* size or more like a full-on Khaleesi *Game of Thrones* level problem here?"

"Inconclusive."

Brandon "Tag" Taggart, a veritable mountain of a man, wore his typical perpetual scowl while shaking his head and looking down at his rifle, "Captain, I would've appreciated a bit more specificity when you said we'd need 'high caliber' from the armory on this."

"We were fresh out of trebuchets and ballistae," muttered Billy.

I brushed his comment aside and turned a handheld tablet around for them to see the profile picture of the man displayed on it. "Eyes up: this is Professor George Metzger. Facility director and priority extract."

Billy squinted at the screen. "He's got a smug face."

"Good thing our squad is the indiscriminate equal opportunity extraction type. The facility is in a remote location, underground. Nothing but Alaskan wilderness for miles around, so chance of civilian collateral damage is minimal. The facility itself went dark six hours ago, and that's our main problem. There's a failsafe triggered by the outage to prevent the escape of any critical materials. At eighteen hours, all entrances into the underground facility will be flash-welded closed and the interior incinerated by an emergency fuel-air system. We'll have two hours after landing to extract Metzger before it goes off. We've done this type of job plenty of times before and, obvious outlying factors notwithstanding, I expect the same excellence in execution."

"If I may, Cap," offered Kelly, "I think our main problem might be the fire-breathing variety. Seems to be a glaring omission on your brief so far. Jokes aside: *can* it breathe fire? How hot does it burn? Mr. Rourke shells out for some top-grade armor, but I'd like to know whether or not that'll matter."

"Metzger and all staff keep everything on closed network. All research, all documents. Everything. Nothing online. That's the other reason for us to go in: extract personnel, as well as all back-up hard drives or physical samples on-site. If we don't pull them or their research out, they'll go up in a puff of smoke as if they'd never existed."

The boys let that hang in the air for a breath. The severity and risk of the job were quelled only by a higher-than-normal occasion for gallows humor. Once more Kelly raised his hand politely to ask a question.

"If we don't know how big it is, do we at least know if it can talk? If so, do you think it'll sound like Benedict Cumberbatch or Sean Connery?"

My face fell into my palm, and I shook my head. Let the boys make their jokes. Better for them to be in good spirits when we finally found out exactly what Rourke had gotten us into. The line between believable and strange tends to get rather blurry in my line of work. This? Yeah. This might just take the damned cake.

Captain Cole West. *Dragon slayer*. What the actual shit...

II.

The jabs kept going for the rest of the flight there. Both Kelly and Billy made a game of seeing who would get under my skin first. I got back at them by maintaining a steady state of professionalism which effectively turned the tables. They also made me realize just how damned ingrained into our culture dragons were.

The pilot came over the line to let me know we were about to start our descent. I signaled back with a thumbs up. My team did some final pre-combat checks on themselves and each other. We switched over from our over-the-ear muffs used for the helicopter to more tactical earbud radios. I tapped the button on mine to sync it to the team and immediately heard Billy's voice.

"You think it'll be European or Asian?" he asked.

I groaned to myself.

"Every movie I've seen they had a British accent. Don't think I've ever heard one speak Chinese?" answered Kelly.

Tag ripped the side-door open as the landing struts hit the deck. We still didn't know whether the facility had gone dark due to hostiles on site or if there was some other catastrophic systems failure at fault, so we stepped off and spread out to cover all angles. The coast was clear.

"No, dumbass," Billy groaned, "like, do you think it'll have whiskers and look like it wants to grant your wish if you collect all seven of its dragon balls, or is it going to be something more medieval with great bat wings like it belongs painted on the side of a dope van?"

"Oh. I don't know. Personally, my favorite's the one Liu Kang turns into in *Mortal Kombat*."

I motioned my team on towards the discreetly hidden bunker elevator entrance, "Going to need you to lower the adorable banter by at least fifteen percent, boys. Besides: Liu Kang didn't turn into a dragon until *Mortal Kombat II*."

The team gave me a collective 'oorah' and I felt everyone's invisible game faces slide into place. They were all professionals at the end of the day. We'd walked through the fire together plenty of times before and collected our fair share of singes and burns along the way.

There was time to laugh, time to joke, and times like right damn now where we needed to get serious.

The entrance to the bunker elevator was sealed with a mighty impressive steel door. Rourke had provided us with a master keycard, and one swipe of it sent the door sliding out of the way on well-oiled rollers. The lift just beyond was bathed in pulsing red emergency lights.

"Could a power outage trigger the failsafe?" Tag asked.

"Unlikely..." I pondered. I found a phone on the wall and put it to my ear. Dead.

The lift ran off the same back-up system as the emergency lights. I was grateful because climbing half a mile's worth of ladders sounded terrible. A quick tap of the button sent us hurtling downwards and I felt gravity launch my stomach up towards my throat. The elevator car gently slowed at the bottom and the doors parted to reveal another heavy blast door similar to the one up top.

The card reader was dead, so I waved Tag over to take care of it. His gigantic physique betrayed the fact that he was an absolute guru when it came to computers and electronics. Tag pulled a small device from his cargo pocket that was no larger than a pack of gum. It was a deceptively powerful remote battery pack that could jumpstart anything from the simple keycard station before us to an entire M1 Abrams.

The brief moment it took Tag to hook it up presented Billy an opportunity to throw out another gibe and he leapt upon it.

"We thinking this is the magic sort of dragon like *Skyrim*," he asked, "or more like a prehistoric species lost to time like from *Reign of Fire*?"

"I'm feeling like a broken record here by saying 'I don't know'," I answered.

"Say it *is* the magic *Skyrim* variety, does the person who kills the dragon get superpowers or not?"

Tag's device lit up green, which I couldn't be more thankful for, and he swiped us in. The steel door rotated out of the way and we found ourselves face-to-face with Professor George Metzger himself. His eyes were wide, frantic.

"Oh, thank God you're here," he said. "They're all dead. *Everyone's* dead!"

III.

"Slow down, Professor," I said. It was directed both at his manic speech and the mad pace that he led us from the elevator deeper into the facility. "You're saying the dragon killed the rest of your staff?"

He shot a look back in my direction that felt like nails on a chalkboard, "Yes. No. Well... indirectly. It's complicated."

"Uncomplicate it," I said. "Clock's against us and I need to understand the situation."

"I believe protocol is for you to follow *my* instructions, not the other way around, Captain West. Mr. Rourke's teams are usually more disciplined."

If the dragon was indeed loose, I had half a mind to feed this prick to it at this point.

"Told you," Billy whispered behind me, "Smug face."

"We've studied it for *years*," Metzger cried. "Nothing like this has ever happened. It was... tamed. Dominated. The specimen was found by accident during a deep geologic survey. It was dormant, in a state of hibernation not unlike estivation among snails. We estimated it had been sleeping for centuries. Rather than risk trying to move it, this facility was constructed around it."

"Get to the part about your staff, professor."

"It got angry," he said simply. "The specimen only showed a brief period of aggression upon first waking and has been compliant since, but yesterday it went berserk out of nowhere."

"What changed? Why'd it find its fight again after all this time?"

"No cause for it," said Metzger. "No change in our routine testing or procedures. My entire staff died from Halon inhalation caused by a malfunction in the fire suppression system. The same fire knocked our main power out. The elevator card reader was inoperable, and I didn't have any way of getting out until you came down."

I weighed everything he was laying down. Berserk dragon, but seemingly no rhyme or reason. To hell with it. At the end of the day, I was a shooter and left the big head-scratching questions to smarter people.

"Professor, do you know where it's gone since it escaped?"

Metzger's face screwed into a puzzled expression, "Escaped...?"

He gestured to an observation window behind him, and all sense in the world disappeared.

IV.

It was the largest animal I'd ever seen. Had to be seventy feet tall from foot to snout, twice that in length if counting its coiled tail. Its onyx scales held an emerald shimmer like a puddle of oil on asphalt. It was definitely what Billy had jokingly called 'the European variety'. But it wasn't the snake-like neck, or the claws, or bat-like digited wings that left me speechless. It was that the dragon was held to a wall with gigantic chains. My guys had joked about all the things the dragon could be, but nobody had guessed this: helpless.

It was all... wrong. Seeing this wondrous creature—its every aspect awe inspiring—utterly dominated like this was not what I had been expecting. It was like seeing the Mona Lisa defaced, or the Statue of Liberty naked and violated. The more I looked and the more I heard the dragon's earth-shaking roars of agony, the more questions arose.

I managed to squeeze a few words through a clenched jaw. "Professor. Talk quick."

Metzger breathed deeply. He placed both palms upon the glass as if taking stock in the dragon for the first time in a long time, or was it that he was taking one last look at it?

"CS-1C: Cryptid Specimen One Charlie. We all took to just calling her Charlie."

"She's a girl?" whispered Kelly, his rifle nearly fell from his hands.

"What she is, is a *goldmine*," said Metzger. "Every inch of her is a material ripe for dedicated advanced projects." He pointed at different parts of the dragon—Charlie—as he continued. "Do you have any idea what we can learn about lightweight aerodynamic fabrics from the wings? How something this *massive* can even be airborne?"

I took a closer look at one of Charlie's wings and noticed the bat-like webbing of her left had been surgically removed. The limb was folded along her backside to hide but twitched weakly.

"The legends abound on the durability of dragon scales," said Metzger. "In this case, myth and reality are one and the same. Harvesting her skin was a delicate process, but the possibilities in body-armor and military vehicle reinforcement are nothing short of revolutionary. Imagine a vest with ten times the protection of traditional Kevlar and only one third the weight. And, frankly, more comfortable. Like a gator-skin vest that could stop bullets."

Metzger's speech fell upon deaf ears as I spotted large patches of Charlie's hide where her scales had been flayed away. The beautiful iridescent greenish onyx shimmer was instead an ugly gray in certain spots. Scar tissue. Huge patchworks of scar tissue like massive canvases along the beast's side.

"See those?" The professor indicated two large metal apparatuses implanted along Charlie's neck just behind her jaw. "Her flaming breath is produced by twin glands on either side of her throat that produce a natural binary incendiary substance. When combined, it combusts upon contact with the air. The substance burns hot enough to melt steel beams, I'll tell you that much. The weapons R&D from it alone would've written the checks to support this facility. We've managed to refine the dragon's incendiary substance into a concentrated resin that has over five times the explosive potential than traditional plastique. I had to increase the extractors after the accident."

I spotted a blackened scorch mark on the ceiling that must've been the cause of the power outage. On the other side of the thick glass, Charlie writhed against the gargantuan restraints around her wrists. There was a twitch in her elongated neck, and then the collar-like apparatus on her throat drained away her fire before she could breathe it. The orange substance was drawn from her glands and through long coiling tubes. It reminded me of a horrific version of those crazy straws you'd get for a soda as a kid. One of Charlie's manacled claws lashed out in frustration, only to be stopped short by the chains. It was then that I saw each digit was scabbed and festering. All the claws had been removed from her right hand. Metzger caught me looking and nodded proudly.

"Yep, we use every part of the buffalo," he beamed. "Individually the scales are nearly unbreakable and the claws are sharp on unbelievable levels. *Atomic* levels, not unlike obsidian. The only difference is, nothing we've tested yet can so much as chip them. That particular research subdivision sort of hit a dead-end in that regard. They haven't yet cracked how to repurpose the claws.

Same goes for the teeth. Most we've managed with either is a middling success with laser etching."

My eyes full upon the bloodied cavities where a few of the stalagmite like teeth were missing from the dragon's jaws. .

"That project is shelved until we can figure out how to break down the teeth or claws, but for now they're at least beautiful mementos. I made that particular piece as a gift for Mr. Rourke," said Metzger. He pointed to a spear on the side wall I'd been too distracted to notice before. It had a five-and-a-half-foot black carbon fiber shaft, but the spearhead was a brilliant white and two-feet in length, obviously made out of one of Charlie's claws. The weapon was nothing short of a beautiful piece. Beautiful, and horrific in its construction.

I dug deep in the recesses of my brain to find the word that captured what I was feeling. The utter opposite of awe. It was a disgust that emptied all warmth, all light, and filled me instead with this undeniable sensation of wrong. This living engine of destruction torn straight from the pages of mythology lay before us a total bastardization of the tales. A thing truly of legend, violated completely and brought so low by man's unending need to exploit, to control, to take. To *use*.

I averted my eyes from the grotesque image, unable to witness anymore. It was a cowardly thing to do, and I was acutely aware of it. Instead, I cast my eyes on the architect of the dragon's torment and somehow forced myself to get back on mission.

"We're nearing the buzzer. Grab what you need."

Metzger directed my men to a collection of hard drives he'd prepped for extraction. He secured the latches on a duralumin case filled with samples and then directed me to a stack of laptops.

"Have your men grab the back-up drives from that room," Metzger said. "I moved my staff there when they died, but please ignore them."

Tag arched an eyebrow in my direction but I brushed away the professor's callous remark. I took to the task of removing the drives from the laptops to try and take my mind away from Charlie's pained roars.

"Don't forget the spear!" Metzger instructed, and I begrudgingly took it off the wall.

I stopped what I was doing to watch as Metzger approached the window.

"It's a shame..." he whispered. "We had so much work left to do. The things we could've accomplished together! But, I have to leave you here, Charlie."

The dragon growled. And something in it sounded *angry*.

V.

The dragon looked through the glass at Metzger and strained against its shackles. And then it did something I'd seen plenty of other animals do when truly desperate: it chewed through its own hand. Fangs tore right through the scales and flesh of its left hand until the entire appendage ripped free. The dragon roared loud enough to shake the walls and then set to freeing its other hand. It pulled against the enormous manacles with everything it had until the metal dug deep between its scales. Still, it pulled. Blood flowed, and it *pulled*. Charlie roared in horror as she degloved the entire hand to escape.

She was loose.

I turned to my men. "Go, go, go! Don't wait for us!"

They ran for the elevator as I latched a hand onto Metzger's shoulder to pull him away from the window. Too late, the dragon's flayed hand punched through the glass and sent both of us to her room below. I hit the ground hard. The recovered hard drives and the grotesque spear Metzger had fashioned both fumbled from my hands.

I hurled myself back onto my feet, then froze in my tracks as I saw Charlie looming over the professor.

Metzger had fancied himself some great conqueror. After all, how could anyone but a *great* man enslave such a powerful creature? Metzger, the master over the dragon. Metzger, the genius. Metzger, the butcher and harvester of its parts. The professor prided himself on these self-attributed titles. And, when he saw the dragon's unrestrained fury free from its chains, he saw every single one of those titles go up in the smoke. See now Metzger the humbled. Witness now Metzger the *terrified*.

Charlie raised her bloody degloved hand and struck him to the ground. If she had wished, she could have pulverized him to mush with ease. Instead she'd smashed at his legs. There are over sixty bones in the lower half of the human body. Metzger felt every single one of them crush in a single instant. Skin, muscle, tendon, and bone were all rendered into a red mash beneath the dragon's paw. The dragon lowered its face over Metzger's own. Reptilian eyes stared mere inches away, and then the beast of legend flung the bisected professor into the air. Its jaws snapped shut around him like a bear trap. Only his head and one arm hung outside of the fangs. The loose morsel slipped from scaled lips, and the snake-like neck snapped out fast as a viper for a follow-up bite to gobble up the remains.

Then, it was just me. On my own. In a massive hangar with one very pissed off and brutalized dragon.

VI.

There was a pause where Charlie took notice of me. It was as if she was gauging what I represented to her. Enemy. Ally. Prey. I saw it all play out across her eyes. I'm sure in her mind anyone who looked like Metzger was just as bad. Couldn't fault her logic. With her one remaining hand she clawed off the metallic collars that had for so long denied her the fire of her own breath. She then raised the bleeding stump of her missing hand to her mouth and belched a burst of flame at the wound to cauterize it.

I've faced death before. Stared down the barrel of a gun. Felt the cold sting of an unfriendly knife against my neck. But when the dragon placed her full attention on me, when I felt the boom of every mighty footfall as she turned in my direction, and when those eyes fixed upon my own, I'd never felt more certain that my time was up.

I held both my hands out to either side plaintively. With one finger I tried to gesture at the door behind her. She looked back at it, then back at me, and I swear she shook her head. I didn't want this fight. Mostly because I didn't stand a snowball's chance in hell. Charlie's face dropped towards the ground so she could get a closer look at me. I expected to see rage in them. A fiery, untameable fury that desired nothing more than to scorch everything around her. Instead, I saw something else. There was a calm in them. They were almost... pleading.

I didn't understand. And then her gaze dropped to my side at where my rifle dangled by its sling. I pointed at it without raising it. I didn't want to mistakenly threaten the beast. She answered with a short puff of flame about her face.

Yes, she seemed to say.

I *didn't* want this fight. But she looked at her burned stump of a hand. She outstretched her ruined wing. Her tongue flicked out between missing teeth. A message spoken without uttering a single word. Dragons were meant to fly. To be mighty and free and powerful. What was a dragon, if she could no longer be any of it? Better to not be at all, if existence meant living as this shell of what you used to be.

Then I understood the choice she was making. If roles were somehow reversed, I suppose I'd want the same thing: freedom, or death. In this instance they would be one and the same for her. One last fight.

"Okay," I said, and reluctantly held my rifle. There was another short puff of fire, and then Charlie lowered to her haunches. Tension loaded in her powerful limbs. A trembling at her throat where she was letting her fire build. No, I didn't want this fight. But, by God, did I feel alive.

You're going to die here, West, I said to myself, *but oh, what a story this will be.*

I raised my weapon and squeezed the trigger as I ran sideways. A battle cry pulled from some ancient field of war ripped forth from my lungs as I fired again and again. The dragon didn't so much as flinch. She rested on her back limbs and put her majesty on full display for me. Both her wings outstretched to either side in what was still, despite her disfigurement, a glorious pose.

Behold, she seemed to say. *See me as I'm meant to be.*

I did. But I did not stop fighting.

She pulled her good wing back and then swung it forward. A mighty whirlwind powerful as a hurricane blew me through the air. I soared for nearly ten feet before tumbling into a heap. The earth beneath me shook as the dragon calmly approached. How many warriors throughout history had challenged her? How many of their charred bones had been forgotten by the ages? It was no wonder she felt no need to rush things. She was the undefeated champion with hundreds of victories under her belt. I was just the latest in a long line of contenders barely worthy of her attention.

I hauled myself up to my feet, eager to try something else. Charlie stopped in her tracks and took a closer curious look at the small object I'd rolled towards her.

An M67 fragmentation grenade packs a little over six ounces of Comp B explosive. It's capable of causing injuries at up to a fifty-foot radius around the detonation and is fatal for everything within fifteen. It went off point-blank against her face and right now I just hoped it would be enough to buy me a few more seconds.

Charlie violently recoiled and pawed at her face. A startled roar bellowed from her throat and she swiped a claw to clear the smoke. I'd already taken that brief moment of reprieve to sprint in a wide circle around her backside.

The gloves were off and the dragon was out for blood now. She took a deep breath in, and then a thick stream of fire burst forth from her mouth. She chased me with it. The flames were just licking at my heels and I ran as fast as I could. I fired another string of bullets at her face, hoping if anything to merely distract her rather than believing they could cause her any pain.

The bullets ricocheted off her scales. They snapped near her eyes, and one finally made her wince, but it was only out of annoyance. Once more she breathed fire in my direction and I was forced to roll out of the way lest I be immolated.

I came out of my roll onto the balls of my feet with my rifle up, only to see that the dragon's fire had coated the end of my gun. Within seconds, the flames melted the steel and I threw it away before the molten metal could burn my hands.

I readied a smoke grenade with one hand while drawing my sidearm with the other. The pistol was utterly useless and I knew it but, goddamn it, I was going to use everything I had. It only took the span of a single breath before I fired the entire magazine dry at her face and had to reload. The heavy .45 caliber rounds did nothing.

Nothing. Metzger had preached about how durable the dragon's scales were. That nothing was strong enough to pierce it. That everything about the dragon was nearly indestructible. The scales, the teeth, the claws, the-

The claws.

I remembered the spear, the one Metzger had fashioned out of one of Charlie's claws as a gift for Mr. Rourke. I looked back to where I'd fallen from the window. There it was. Possibly the only object in existence which could pierce the dragon's skin. The only problem was that it was a good fifty yards away.

Yeah, I took my chances.

I dropped the smoke grenade behind me and made a mad dash for the spear. There's a unique form of terror that comes with being chased by an animal. It's... primal. Many a man fleeing a rabid dog has understood this. Unarmed hikers chased by cougars have felt it. Wandering campers run afoul of a bear have learned of this fear. It's a fear so ancient and eternal, it trumps nearly all others.

What I felt was not anything like that. This was not an animal pursuing me. This was a force of nature. I was a tiny little man who thought he could outrun a living storm. A maelstrom of razor teeth and swirling flames. The number of ways the dragon could end me were dizzying. Burned alive. Smashed to paste. Ripped to pieces. Swallowed hole. So many ways to go, none of them pleasant in the slightest.

Thing is, I wasn't thinking of a single one of them. I was thinking about how the spear was now just ten feet away.

I didn't dare to look behind me. To see death incarnate approaching? Yeah, I didn't need the chance of tripping over my bootlaces. But I heard her roar bellowing past her fangs. I felt the floor beneath my feet shake as her clawed hand stomped after me. I could smell the fire building in her maw behind me. Teeth. Claws. Fire. All weapons at her disposal.

And now I had my own. My momentum carried me into a slide and I snatched the spear up in my hands at the same second I felt the hot breath of the dragon as it lunged to tear me apart in its jaws. I rose to face the dragon with spear gripped tight in hand as it bore down upon me. Her jaws closed around my entire body. Razor-sharp teeth shredded through the armor around my shoulder and torso as the dragon bit down, the flames began to belch forth from its throat---

And stopped abruptly short as the spearhead spiked through the roof of the dragon's mouth. I felt it go deep, past flesh, through skull, and enter the base of the brain.

The two of us stood very still for that moment. If the dragon finished closing her jaws it would act like a guillotine of daggers around my body, but it would send the spear piercing the rest of the way through her brain. There was a violent tremble that ran through the beast's body, and I felt her weight shift back.

I jerked the spear free. The length of the blade was drenched in blood and flames. My own blood soaked my torso from a dozen lacerations where her fangs had dragged against my flesh. The dragon snorted, coughed an ugly cough, and breathed out a mouthful of blood rather than flames. Slowly, so slowly, the dragon settled to the ground upon its belly.

I remained frozen on the spot. Chest heaving. Face dripping sweat, body dripping blood. The flames danced along the tip of the spear where it had pierced the dragon's body. A sound came forth from Charlie's jaws. Not a roar. Not a hiss. It was almost a whimper. A huff of resignation. Thousands of battles against thousands of challengers, but here she was finally at peace. At the end.

The spear felt very heavy in my hands as I walked alongside the length of her neck to look into her eyes. Despite the reptilian slit in them, there was something so human in their expression. I'd watched the lights go out in many a man's eyes over the years. Some lights go out in a wink, some dim slowly. The dimming ones hurt the most to watch. This was no different.

Her one remaining hand twitched and I feared she was going to take one final desperate swipe at me. Instead, she pointed with a single claw at a spot just behind her jaws.

The flame glands.

The beast blinked slowly in acceptance.

I readied the spear, its end still wreathed in flames, and took a breath. I hadn't wanted this fight. That it was about to end did not change that one damned bit.

A scream escaped me all on its own as I thrust forward with the spear. I put everything I had behind it. The flaming tip easily penetrated through the scales, and there was a brief flare that flashed out and made me shield my eyes. The reptilian slit in her eye contracted for a second as I delivered the killing blow, then the pupil relaxed and expanded. Charlie breathed her last breath, and every other muscle in her body went slack.

Once more I pulled the spear from the dragon's body. Her own burning substance flowed into her veins, the glowing lines weaved crisscross throughout her body, and the fires rose, not in a violent explosion, but in a somber funeral pyre. One that only I stood before to witness. There was a sound like a great forest settling as she was consumed to nothing but bones and ash.

The klaxon blare of the facility's alarm snapped me back to the moment. Time was running out, and my boys were good enough to follow my orders *not* to come back for me. Which meant that if I didn't get a move on quick then

I would have the rest of a very limited life to appreciate the dragon's remains. My radio earbud squawked as if on cue.

"Cap, we're at the elevator holding it for you and the Professor," said Billy. "I know the squad's overdue for some bonding time, but all the same I'd prefer not getting permanently sealed underground with you."

"Professor didn't make it," I said, and hefted the spear over my shoulder. "I'm en route."

"Rog, we'll hold here long as we can."

I stepped off to run for the exit lift, when I skidded to a halt passing the dragon's ashen remains. There was something out of place among the piles of gray ash and clean white bones that caught my eye. And I knew exactly what it was the second I spotted it.

'What changed? Why'd she find her fight again after all this time?'

The clock was running dangerously low, yet still I spared precious seconds approaching the scattered bones. I plunged both hands deep into the ash and blew out a deep breath to clear them away. It swirled away from my hands to reveal what was hidden underneath.

An egg. Shimmering onyx and emerald just as Charlie's scales had been. It was warm to the touch, and surprisingly heavy. The weight felt significant in more ways than one. I considered for a moment, and placed the egg back amidst the ashes.

The facility would be sealed shut. Who knows for how long? Decades, centuries maybe before anyone would discover the entrance. Longer still before someone decided to crack it back open. A long while indeed before any man would possibly come exploring in these depths to discover its buried secrets. Maybe the egg will still be dormant by then. Or, like its mother, perhaps it'll have hatched long ago and simply been waiting.

I took one last look at the egg and then left to rejoin my team. I prayed silently as I ran, hoping that humanity could change in time.

Maybe, just maybe, the people who found the dragon next time would be different than the last group.

"He who fights too long against dragons becomes a dragon himself; and if you gaze too long into the abyss, the abyss will gaze into you."

— Friedrich Nietzsche

Unauthorized
Pam Ahlen

Every act of creation is first an act of destruction
— Picasso

Sprayed wild on a wall
at the corner of Second and Main,
a real piece—
as in
masterpiece,
as in
ten-foot dragon
screaming green,
as in
worthy of Saint George—
this Raphael of the Street
that ignites its mighty blaze,
flames our desire—
as in
see me breathe my fire,
live my life out loud.

Come Not Between
Erica Ruppert

"I hate camping," Paula said, wrapping her hands around the warm metal mug. "If it weren't for you, I'd never be out here."

Mallery looked into the fire. "I thought you liked it out in nature."

Paula moved closer to him. "I do. I like being out here with you. I just hate camping."

He shifted away from her. "It's not even cold yet," he said.

"Don't be like that," Paula said. "I'm here, aren't I?"

He relented, and slung an arm around her shoulder. "Be glad the Draconids start in October. It'll be worse in February, when the next shower comes."

He pressed his head against hers, and spoke into her ear like he was telling a secret. "Years ago there used to be hundreds, even thousands of outbursts in an hour. But it's been quieter, for a while now. The moon has been too bright."

Paula sighed, then put the mug at her feet and leaned forward to stir the fire.

"And this is the first day of the meteor showers," she said, looking up.

"Yes," Mallery said. "Like I said, it usually goes on for four or five days, but we'll only be here for three. That should let us see the best of it."

Paula nodded. A streak of light skimmed across the sky.

"There," Mallery said. "They're starting."

"Tell me the story again," she said. "While we watch the meteors."

Mallery snuggled up to her before beginning.

"The constellation Draco never sets. It's always in the northern sky. See, there?" Mallery said, pointing into the deep night. "That's Draco. And that star, in its tail, used to be the pole star. Thuban."

"There are too many stars," Paula said. "I don't know which one you want me to see."

"Follow my finger," Mallery said, his voice tinged with quick annoyance. "The bright one, there, near the North Star. My mother used to say the dragon saw the sailors staring at it, and moved away from them. But sometimes it gets curious and comes down to look back."

Paula shook her head and put her hands between her knees.

"I'm cold," she said. "And I can't see it."

"I thought you wanted me to tell the story," he said.

Paula settled against him and closed her eyes. "I'm sorry," she said. "I do."

Mallery drew a slow breath.

"Thuban was the pole star to the ancient Egyptians. They built their pyramids to face it, so they could enter the huge tombs by starlight." he continued, his voice soft again. "It's brighter than our sun, but so far away you can't tell. Someday, when the dragon finishes turning it will be the pole star again. But that will be many, many centuries from now, because stars move so slowly."

***

In Paula's dreams the eye, the great white star, shone on her, burning her skin until she could see her own charred bones, no dragon fire but the engine of a sun. It came down as it had come down a thousand times, a million, in a cycle too wide for her to see its whole pattern. She still knew it was pattern repeating. And it was her turn to appear in it.

She sat up, sticky with sweat and sure she was on fire. Then she was awake, and her panic faded to confusion and unease.

Mallery half-roused and reached for her.

"You okay?" he mumbled.

Paula swallowed hard against the sour taste in her mouth, but it still swam around her tongue. She wanted to spit.

"Yeah, I'm okay," she said. "Just a bad dream."

***

Paula brought the remains of their dinner back to the car to keep it from drawing bears, and stood for a while in the quiet darkness. Behind her she could just hear Mallery tidying the campsite and feeding the fire. She looked up at all the stars and the few bright trails of the meteors. As she watched, a blank space swept over the scattered lights and shut them out like a drawn curtain. Then it was gone and the stars shone down again.

She watched, waiting for the blackness to come again.

"Everything all right?" Mallery called.

"Just trying to find Thuban," she answered, turning her eyes to the ground and walking back to him.

By the fire, the stars shone far less sharply.

"How long have we been together, now?" he asked her as she settled beside him on the log.

She reached for his hand and laced her fingers through his.

"Three months and some days," she said.

"I feel like I've known you forever," he said.

Paula smiled with a small shake of her head, and drew her hand away.

"Don't be so much, Mal," she said. "Thank you for bringing me up here with you."

"You're the first person I've ever asked to come with me," he said.

Even in the golden firelight she could see him blush. He tried to smile, but his eyes were serious.

"Do you want to hear another story?" Mallery asked.

"Is it about another constellation?" she responded, her voice falsely light.

Mallery only stared at her, unhappy with her tone, until she looked away.

"I'm sorry. Tell me," she said.

Mallery smiled, then. He pressed his lips against her hair and nuzzled her ears before he sat back and began.

"It's something else I've never shared with anyone," he said. "My mother said our family has always fought the dragon. We drove it up and kept it in the sky."

"The dragon? Draco? How?" Paula asked. .

Mallery shrugged. "However. Spears, swords, guns, I guess."

"But it's just a bunch of stars."

"It's more than that. Sometimes, the light becomes a real thing. This is what the myths are about."

Paula waited for a few seconds, deciding how far to follow.

"How do they know where to go, where the dragon will go? Is it just luck? Are there signs?" she asked at last.

Mallery shook his head.

"I'm not sure. My mother never explained it very well. I don't think she really knew, either." he said. "I think the dragon can scent us, somehow. My mother did say if we don't meet it and drive it away when it comes, it will hunt whoever it finds instead, and they won't know how to stop it."

Paula closed her eyes for a moment, thinking as she listened.

"She said the dragon would know our family, though." he went on. "That its first goal is always to come after one of us."

Paula opened her eyes and looked at him, and started to say something. But she shut her mouth, and changed her mind.

"What?" Mallery prodded.

Paula hesitated. It didn't matter. "How long is always?"

Mallery laughed.

"Always is thousands of years, back to the ancient Greeks and Egyptians."

"So," she said slowly. "Is that even the same family, then? I mean, does a bloodline persist over that much time, that you could still call the same family? It would branch out, I think. Like the legend of how many descendants Genghis Kahn has."

"Wow," Mallery said roughly. "That's a weird response."

A knot in a burning log popped, throwing out a burst of sparks that floated up to meet the shooting stars.

Paula shrugged. She was in it, now.

"There's more to family than just a name, but that's how we always seem to define it, isn't it? I mean, it's not like your ancestors all married close relatives to preserve the bloodline, right? It all got spread out over the years, just a drop left in so many different people. We could be related, for all you know."

Mallery stared into the fire, his jaw tightening.

Meteors fell through the dark sky like arrows of light.

"My *family*," he said at last, "fought the dragon whenever it would come down to earth."

A gust of wind flattened the flames into sheets before they sprang back up.

"Okay," Paula said, softly. "When's the last time it came down?"

He looked at her from the corner of his eye.

"About a hundred and fifty years ago. My great-great-great grandfather drove it back up."

A stick snapped somewhere behind them. Leaves rustled as something moved away from them, deeper into the woods. Mallery turned to look, but the dark beneath the trees was too thick.

"How?" she asked.

He sighed.

"With a weapon he inherited, made of metal from a meteor."

"Did all your family have weapons like that, then?"

Mallery held his hands out to the fire. Paula was aware of just how far he had withdrawn from her.

"I don't know," he said. "Probably not all of them."

"Do you have the one from your however-great grandfather? Did you inherit it?"

Mallery stood up and stretched hard.

"Enough stories," he said. "I'm going to sleep. Enjoy the light show."

Paula sat alone until the fire burned down. When she was sure Mallery was asleep, she banked the hot embers in ash and crawled into the tent beside him.

Through the thin fabric wall she listened to the night moving all around them, wondering what the wind let move behind it, what she wasn't able to hear.

**

Paula thought she lay awake in the warm shroud of her sleeping bag. The tent hid the sky from her, but she didn't need to see it. She knew what was there, what travelled through the cold reaches above her. What saw her. What knew who she was.

Typhon, Ladon, Asterius. The Greeks gave the dragon many names. It answered to them all.

Paula held a sword as bright as the flare of a meteor burning, weightless in her hand but not bright enough to ward away the great dragon that was coming for her. The wind of its wings buffeted her as it bore down. The sword became a length of twisted wood before it dissolved in her grasp. She struggled to stay on her feet, and then she was falling free in the sky, the earth gone from under her.

Mallery shook her awake. She grunted and swatted at him, but he unzipped her sleeping bag to let the cold air in.

"What's the matter with you?" she said, sitting up and wrapping her arms around herself. She was still dizzy from dreaming.

"Draco is moving faster," Mallery said. "It's picking up speed. I can see it. This is it. It's coming down from the sky."

"What are you talking about?" she said. "It can't."

Half-awake, she knew she was lying. She wondered how much he really knew.

Stars move slowly, she thought.

But dragons move fast.

"It did," Mallery insisted. He pulled something out from beneath his folded blankets.

"Stay here. This is what I told you. This is what my family has always done."

"Mallery–" she began.

"Shut up. Stay here. It might not notice you at all if you don't move."

And he was gone into the cold night, the tent opening flapping behind him.

She wriggled free of her sleeping bag and followed.

At first she couldn't see him. Without the campfire, the stars lit the sky with a white sheen against the depths of measureless space, the shapes it illuminated becoming strange in the pale light. Then Mallery raised a long pole into the air, and she recognized him. She darted across the clearing to join him.

"You can't do this alone," she said, as she reached his side.

"Be quiet," he hissed, then froze.

"There," he said softly, lifting his chin toward the sky.

She looked up, and held her breath.

The stars moved. Something had turned its head and seen them where they stood, uncounted miles below. Something would come, now, fast. As fast as light that had been travelling for millennia already. Faster than anything that lived should be. All the memories roiling her dreams came crashing through.

"Get out of here," Mallery said, shoving Paula suddenly away from him.

She stumbled and grabbed onto him, swinging him in a circle. The pole he held struck her above her ear as he tried to keep his balance. Her head rang but she still snatched at the pole. He angled it out of her reach, then pulled free of her and pushed her toward the black shadow of the trees.

She held onto him, dragging him with her, wrestling for his weapon.

"I have to fight it," he said. "Get away from here. Run."

"No," Paula said. She had to make him know what she had learned from her own mother. "You have it wrong. You're the bait."

If he heard her, he didn't understand.

"The bloodline. The family. There are so many of us. Some draw it out, and some fight it. I'm the one who will fight this time. *You are the bait.*"

Mallery's eyes were white in the starlight. He bared his teeth as he began to make sense of what she was telling him. For a moment he seemed completely unaware of the beast above them, coming down like a lightning strike.

"Get away from me," he growled, pulling the staff free of her grasping hands and bringing it down to jab her hard in the chest.

She staggered back, gasping for breath.

"You damned liar," he spat, and spun away from her to meet the dragon.

Her skin prickled with an animal awareness. There was no more time to argue.

She let him have the staff, and ran.

***

Paula crouched in the shelter of the crowded trees that circled the clearing, and watched the sky. Far above where Mallery stood, a sweep of stars disappeared, as if something blocked their light. A mass of blackness fell over him, the burning light within it an eye as bright as the pole star tilted toward the earth.

For a moment, Mallery was frozen in that light, a black stick figure held against the white heat of a sun. The wind of the dragon's descent rattled and tossed the branches around Paula, wrenching weak ones loose. Mallery fought to stand before the gusts, lifting the staff to meet the onslaught. She watched as Mallery stumbled, fell to his knees, rose again. He swung the staff over his head at the impossible thing that materialized just out of his reach.

The dragon's head dipped down to examine Mallery's threat, close enough that even among the trees Paula could smell the icy dust of its breath. Its shining eye gazed at Mallery like a searchlight turned on him, too bright to look into. Then the serpent fell upon him, its long, glittering body stretching between earth and space. A swath of solid darkness followed as the great wings belled and blotted out the stars, sweeping Mallery across the field like a puppet. She saw the dragon's jaws open, wide, wider, until the great black maw was all of the world, and the serpent's cold breath finally knocked Mallery to the ground. The long, long teeth came down around him, as delicate as frost, sinking into the ground, carving trenches as they slowly drew together. He lay with the frozen earth rutching beneath him, trapped in their cage.

Paula heard his ragged breathing through the utter silence the dragon brought with it. She heard his whimpers. She would whimper, too, if she had to lay there waiting for the sky to swallow her whole.

And then the beast snapped its jaws shut on the earth, on the frail body between its glistening fangs. It tossed its head and swallowed the mud and mortal clay, its frozen scales rippling as its long throat worked. Then it opened its mouth again and spat something out.

The staff Mallery had wielded clattered to the ground, ringing where it struck rock..

The dragon hovered in the clearing, a chasm of darkness within the enormous night, casting about like a great hound. It knew she was there, but hadn't found her, yet. Even in the shine of the distant stars, she could not see it clearly. It filled too much of the sky, absorbed too much of the light, changed and swelled and shrank as it moved like silt in water. It was an alien thing here, not bound by earthly rules.

But then a glimmer of starlight bent around the dragon's shifting form and picked out the long shape of the staff, as if to make certain she saw it.

Paula waited, counting her heartbeats, until the dragon turned its bright, bright eye away. She waited a second more and then ran as fast as she could drive herself over the uneven ground, toward the swirling bulk of the monster, toward the weapon she needed. As her fingers closed around the cold metal, the dragon saw her and roared, its voice a void, an absence, sucking in all sound. The light of its attention fell on her like stones. She wanted to scream to break the awful silence, but knew her voice would be lost in the emptiness. She bit down on her terror and stood her ground.

As the dragon bent to strike, Paula hefted the long iron pole and found its balance. It tingled in her hands, like a live wire. Sure of her aim, she spun the staff up into the air and connected with the dragon's side. She gasped, shocked that the serpent had substance inside the uncertainty of it. The pole rattled from her grasp, her arm numb from the impact. Chips of ice flew like sparks where she had struck it, and for a maddening moment she could see what chaos lay inside the dragon's skin. She did scream, then, and shut her eyes against the raw pain of having seen.

The dragon beat its vast wings, and the sudden wave of air pressure knocked her down. The beast rose, away from her.

She huddled where she fell, forcing her eyes to open again, forcing herself to be calm, watching the dragon's shadow move across the sky to circle far out of her reach.

She had hurt it. She had driven it back.

It hadn't expected that.

A shooting star cut across the sky, showing where the serpent no longer was.

She wondered if the dragon would ever remember how they fought. She wondered if its huge, ancient mind could hold a thought as small as the memory of her. If something so monstrous could think at all, or if every time it was struck it was surprised anew.

She shuddered, unable to control the fear that swept through her.

At least Mallery had been spared that much.

Above her, as high as the heavens, the great serpent twined in the endless darkness, the shape of its body picked out in shards of light. It circled in wider and wider gyres, its bright, shining eye visible as it approached Polaris.

Paula climbed to her feet and raised the iron staff in an unsteady fist, and felt it pull toward the old pole star.

She knew the dragon felt the pull, too.

It would come to hunt again.

And someone else would hold the weapon when the pattern repeated.

Drakaina by Amanda Bergloff

KNOW YOUR DRAGONS
An Identification Guide for the Beginner

Dragons are known all over the world and are endemic to all cultures, myth, and legend. In the Bible, Genesis 1:21 states "God created great whales." The Hebrew word translated "whales" is everywhere else translated as "dragon" or "great serpent." The Holy Quran (sūrat al-Kahf, verses 93–98) may refer to dragons, according to some scholars. Buddhists consider them symbols of wisdom and protection. Taoists look on them as symbols of their faith.

The wide variety of,. and disparate attitudes toward, these creatures make it difficult for the beginning student to differentiate between them, and to that end we present the following guide.

Although appearing in many colors and even multi-hued at times, generally speaking, there are only a few types of dragons. From least intelligent to most, these are:

BEASTS – Single-minded, brutal, and selfish. They can vary in appearance from serpentine to bipedal to quadrupedal, winged or wingless. They are the most common encountered.

WURMS (or WYRMS) – Purpose-driven and ruthless. These are most found guarding a treasure, location, or person. These may have more than one head, breathe fire or other elements, and seldom move from their station.

ANCIENTS – Wisest and most intelligent, they avoid human contact and go out of their way to find hiding places nearly impossible to access without the ability to fly. Winged, sometime two- or four-legged, they cannot be controlled except by the strongest magic or ancient enchants and weapons.

Western World Dragons

Best known to the Western world is the evil, fire-breathing dragon. This fearsome creature usually inhabits caves on mountain sides and attacks at a whim if not mollified by some form of sacrifice, traditionally a virgin maiden. This image is relatively new compared to the Eastern dragons (see below) and is generally attributed to ancient Greek and Roman legends. Most famous of these is the Hydra defeated by Heracles.

Less well known is the story that the great Tiber flood that decimated Rome in 589 AD was caused by a river dragon who sent her progeny to harass the population.

"My deacon (Agiulf) told me that the previous year, in the month of November, the River Tiber had covered Rome with such flood-water that a number of ancient churches had collapsed and the papal granaries had been

destroyed, with the loss of several thousand bushels of wheat. A great school of water-snakes swam down the course of the river to the sea, in their midst a tremendous dragon as big as a tree-trunk, but these monsters were drowned in the turbulent salt sea-waves and their bodies were washed up on the shore"
(Gregory of Tours, *History of the Franks*, X.1).

More recently, the Native American tribes knew of dragons as well. The Seneca, for instance, believed in a dragon that inhabited the rivers and lakes of Canada called Gaasyendietha. Better known is Quetzalcoatl, the winged serpent of the Aztecs.

This is only one of numberless stories from medieval times tell of dragons thundering across history, wreaking chaos wherever they go. Once one travels west of the Levant, the image of the dragon begins to take on its darker nature. The Egyptian dragon Apep, although more of form like a snake, is considered to be the enemy of Ra and the Lord of Chaos.

Eastern World Dragons

The attitude toward dragons in the Middle and Far East is much different from the West. In general, dragons represent good luck, wisdom, and fertility, although there are exceptions. As far back as the Xinglongwa culture of China (6200-5400 BC), the dragon has been featured in art and tradition.

One Persian belief concerned the Azhdaha, a great serpent. Eating its heart was said to convey courage and bravery, its skin can heal a broken heart, and the soil in which its head is buried becomes rich and fertile. Various writers described how heroes of old defeated several of these creatures.

In India, there is a deified dragon named Pakhangba, dating from the Kangleipak civilization of (1500 BC – 1891 AD) the Manipur region. He is recognized throughout India, Bangladesh, and even Myanmar as bringing peace and tranquility.

Southeast Asia is filled with tales of dragons and serpents, most of which are tied to natural elements or events. Seasonal changes, rain, wind, even the movement of clouds, are all supposedly under their control.

Proceeding further eastward, we come to the Chinese dragons, of which there are several types. The majority of these are beneficent, usually associated with water or rain. However, each of the four elements (earth, water, fire, air) does have its own dragon associated. How they are viewed and what their particular powers may be vary from location to location and to list them all would take many books to contain. The most important seems to be the Yellow Dragon. As the manifestation of the Yellow Emperor, the center of the universe, it rules over the rest of its type.

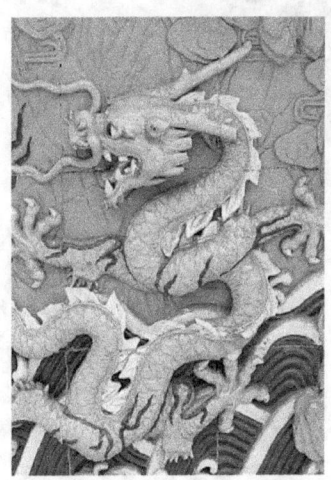

The Chinese culture depends heavily on manifestations of ancient creatures like dragons, listing them among phoenix and qilin as most important.

Lastly, we move to the Pacific and find here the most fascinating of all dragons, the Filipino Bakunawa. Said to be responsible for eclipses, rain, earthquakes, and other natural disasters, it has been a part of the Cebuano island culture for millennia.

The story is that in the beginning there were seven moons, one for each night, and the earth was full of light even after the sun went down. The great god Bathala created them to ensure prosperity and happiness while he slept. The dragon Bakunawa saw the beautiful moons and wanted them, so it devoured each one in turn until only one remained. As it went to eat the last moon, the people came out and made a great noise to awaken Bathala, who saved the last moon from being eaten at the last second.

Even until today, people will come out of their homes and pound on pots and pans to scare off Bakunawa from eating the moon if there is an eclipse. A calendar was created to follow its movement.

In Japan, the dragon is called Ryu and its kind is ruled by the god Ryujin. They are most associated with wisdom, luck, and strength. The symbol of the Fuku Ryu is associated with good luck just as is the uplifted trunk of the Indian god Ganesh. It is the favorite of all Japanese dragons, for obvious reasons.

Painting by Tija86

The Dragon Fascination

It should be obvious that the attraction dragons hold on us extends far beyond mere national or cultural boundaries. There is something that reaches deeper into our collective psyche to titillate or terrify. Some maintain that they represent the unknown and target our primordial fear of it. Some think they represent mystery and tweak our imagination. More than likely, it is much more complicated.

Dragons represent different things to different people, but in the end, they are the embodiment of our fears and our joys, the repository of what our minds relate to reality and unreality. They bridge that gap between imagination and substance, and so they will always fascinate.

"How should we be able to forget those ancient myths that are at the beginning of all peoples, the myths about dragons that at the last moment turn into princesses; perhaps all the dragons of our lives are princesses who are only waiting to see us once beautiful and brave. Perhaps everything terrible is in its deepest being something helpless that wants help from us."

— Rainer Maria Rilke, *Letters to a Young Poet*

CREDITS

Unauthorized (poem)
Pamela Ahlen is a former music educator from South Florida who moved with her husband to Vermont to escape strip malls. She is Special Events Coordinator for Osher Life Long Learning Institute at Dartmouth and compiled and edited its *Anthology of Poets and Writers: Celebrating Twenty-Five Years at Dartmouth.* She received an MFA in creative writing from Vermont College of Fine Arts and is the author of the poetry chapbook *Gather Every Little Thing* (Finishing Line Press) and the chapbook *Getting it Down on Paper, Shaping a Friendship* (Orchard Street Press) in collaboration with poet Anne Bower.

Drakaina (art)
Amanda Bergloff is a graphic designer and digital/mixed media artist of the weirder things in life. Her cover art has been published by the Jules Verne Society's **Extraordinary Visions** Anthology, *Utopia Science Fiction,* and *The Fairy Tale Magazine,* as well as interior illustrations for Horrorsmith Publishing, *The Sprawl Magazine, Enchanted Conversation,* and other publications. She lives in Denver, Colorado and is a shameless collector of books, toys, and comics.

Dragon's Lament (short story)
Michael P Coglan is a fantasy and science fiction writer, a poet specializing in haiku, and an all around nerd. He lives in Iowa with his cosplaying wife and their two dogs, Ripley and Gimli.

Voyage of the Dragon Song (poem)

Anna Dallara is a filmmaker and speculative fiction writer from North Carolina. She holds a Bachelor of Arts in Classics and a Master's in Information Science from the University of North Carolina at Chapel Hill, where she wrote her thesis on applications of artificial intelligence. Her work has appeared in *The Dread Machine*. Follow her at *Anna's Journal* on YouTube, where she documents the process of building a creative life.

Stage Magic **(short story)**
Karen Eisenbrey (she/her) lives in Seattle, WA, where she leads a quiet, orderly life and invents stories to make up for it. Karen writes fantasy and science fiction novels, as well as short fiction and the occasional poem or song if it insists. Published books include sci-fi workplace rom-com/survival story *Ego & Endurance*; the **Daughter of Magic** fantasy trilogy; **St. Rage** garage-rock/superhero series; and **A Quest for Hidden Things (Tales from Deep River Book 1)**, coming from Not A Pipe Publishing in 2024. Karen shares her life with her husband, two young adult sons, and four feline ghosts.

Gladys and the Iguana Incident **(short story)**
David Hankins is the award-winning author of **Death and the Taxman**. He writes from the thriving cornfields of Iowa where he lives with his wife, daughter, and two dragons disguised as cats. His writing journey began in the oral tradition of convincing his daughter to Go To Sleep with inventive stories. That usually backfired. After years of Just One More Story, David began transcribing his midnight ramblings in an attempt to keep his storylines straight. Children are ruthless in identifying mistakes in fairy tales. David writes lighthearted speculative fiction because that's what he loves to read and—this is the important bit—there's not nearly enough

humor in the world. David aims to change that, one story at a time.

David joined the US Army after college and, through some glitch in the bureaucracy, convinced Uncle Sam to fund his wanderlust for twenty years. He has lived in and traveled through much of Europe, central Asia, and the United States. Now that he's retired from the Army, David devotes his time to his passions of writing, traveling, and finding new ways to pay his mortgage.

David's short stories have graced the pages of **Writers of the Future** Volume 39, *Amazing Stories, DreamForge Magazine,* and others.

Snowborn (short story)

Andrew Knighton is an author of short stories, comics, and the fantasy novellas *Ashes of the Ancestors* and *Silver and Gold*. As a freelance writer, he's ghostwritten over forty novels in other people's names, as well as articles, history books, and video scripts. He lives in Yorkshire with an academic and a cat, growing vegetables and dreaming about a brighter future. His novel *The Executioner's Blade*, set in the same world as *Snowborn*, will be published by Northodox Press in February 2025, and you can find more of his work, including related flash fiction, at andrewknighton.com.

Cover Art

Tony Kurbanali is a digital artist and illustrator who lives in San Francisco, California. He is originally from the West Indies, the island of Trinidad in the Caribbean then moved to Escondido, California as a teen. As a child, he loved comics and started copying the superhero characters he saw in those books. He attended Palomar Junior College in San Marcos, California, and received an Associate of Arts in Commercial Art and Illustration.

After moving to San Francisco, Tony attended California College of the Arts. His final thesis portfolio was titled 'Terror and the Supernatural.' This body of work was inspired by the short stories of such authors as Edgar Allan Poe, Richard Matheson, Robert Bloch, and Ambrose Bierce, to name a few.

His influences in art are varied and include John Singer Sargent, George Bellows, Thomas Eakins, Burne Hogarth, Norman Lindsay, Robert George Harris, Robert McGinnis, Frank Frazetta, Bron, and pulp-era artists like Norman Saunders. There are contemporary concept artists that he is also influenced by.

Tony is ever inspired by the history and atmosphere of San Francisco which helps his constant pursuit and growth of his art.

Dragon (art)

Stephen Lillie is a professional illustrator and cartoonist with too many years experience. He has worked on a wide variety of projects including everything from medical diagrams, magazine covers, political cartoons to fantasy and science fiction. Published in many counties around the world, but mostly in The United Kingdom. The majority of his work history has been editorial and educational.

Most images are created with a combination of traditional and digital media. Passionate about line and expression. A compulsive mark-maker he enjoys experimenting with new media and pen nibs.

After years of living in London, he recently moved to Wales, but still exhibits in London

The Care and Feeding of Banzai Dragons (short story)

Raised on a healthy diet of creature double features and classic SF TV, **Gregory L. Norris** writes short stories, novellas, novels, and the occasional script for television and film. He once worked as a screenwriter on two episodes of Paramount's *Star Trek: Voyager* and pens the Gerry Anderson's **The Day After Tomorrow: Into Infinity** novels for Anderson Entertainment in the UK based on the classic NBC made-for-TV movie, which he watched and loved as a boy. In October, his novel **Monsterland** debuts from the fine folks at Van Velzer Press, his fifth release with the company. His most recent is the hilarious, soapy paranormal, **Desperate Housewolves.**

Born Hungry (poem)

Rachel Nussbaum is a writer and artist from the Big Island of Hawaii. She's loved dragons since she was a kid and would ask her mom to rent *The Flight of Dragons* on VHS every chance she could.

Rachel's short stories and poetry have been featured in many anthologies, including *The Mammoth Book of Dieselpunk* from Running Press and *Crash Code* from Blood Bound Books. Her debut novella *We Rotted in the Bitterlands* came out in 2021 from Mannison Press, and will hopefully be the first of many more longform projects for her. Rachel currently resides in the Bay Area, where she hopes to grow her creative career and one day write and illustrate her own novels and comics. There will absolutely be dragons involved.

At Night (art)

Angela Patera is a published writer and artist, and an emerging poet. Her short stories have appeared in Livina Press, *Myth & Lore Zine*, and more. Her art has appeared in numerous publications, as well as on the cover of Selenite Press, *Penumbra Online, Monster Mag*, and *Apothecary Journal*. When Angela isn't creating, she likes to spend time outside in nature. You can find her on both Twitter/X and Instagram @angela_art13

Stained Glass Dragon (poem)
Katherine Quevedo was born and raised near Portland, Oregon, where she works as an analyst and lives with her husband and two sons. Her poetry has been nominated for the Pushcart Prize and the Rhysling Award, and her debut mini-chapbook, *The Inca Weaver's Tales*, is available from Sword & Kettle Press. Her poems have appeared in *Asimov's*, *Heroic Fantasy Quarterly*, *Old Moon Quarterly*, *The Sprawl Mag*, *TOWER Magazine*, and elsewhere. When she isn't writing, she enjoys watching movies, playing old-school video games, singing, belly dancing, and making spreadsheets.

Fire Dragon (art)
Brian Malachy Quinn uses watercolors, pen and ink, digital media, block prints, and etchings. He was a research scientist, then taught Physics at University for ten years, now he works as an analyst in the investment field - though his passion is art. He longs for the day when he can do art full time. As an artist he has won twenty-two international art awards in juried competitions in the last twenty-four months, in the last five years, he has sold forty-four illustrations, including twenty-four covers - three commissioned. He has always created art since early childhood. His style can be surreal for speculative fiction or literary fiction, or realistic for his fallback of lion paintings. He is compelled to create art and does so every day and finds it as a way to put aside his worries and stresses and produce "good brain chemicals". He lives with his family including his two rescue cats: Sebastian and Missy in Ohio.

The Nocturnal (art)
Sonali Roy is a freelance writer taking interest in holistic approaches for maintaining good health both for

humans and their nonhuman friends, business management, latest science discoveries, health & medicine, technology, robotics, archaeology, architecture, food & nutrition, history, astronomy, spirituality, unexplained, and art & culture. Besides, she's a passionate traveler & photographer, music composer, singer, painter, 3-D art designer and practices yoga & meditation regularly. Devoted to vegan diet, she enjoys creative writing. Sonali is accompanied by the sweet memories of her 8-yr old canine friend Fuchoo, who left her forever last year.

Come Not Between (short story)

Erica Ruppert, HWA, SFWA. lives in northern New Jersey with her husband and too many cats. Her short stories have appeared in magazines including *Vastarien, Lamplight,* and *Nightmare,* on podcasts including *PodCastle,* and in multiple anthologies. Her debut collection, *Imago and Other Transformations,* was released by Trepidatio Publishing in March 2023. When she is not writing, she runs, bakes, and gardens with more enthusiasm than skill.

Dragon Tapestry (art)

Richard E Schell works in the biomedical field in California. He enjoys writing and has published over 100 articles and other works in both the biomedical field as well as in fictional genres and poetry. He enjoys photography, literature and travel. He also volunteers in animal rescue.

Dragon Dream (poem)

Kerstin Schulz has a degree in Anthropology from Grinnell College and pursued graduate work in Folklore at the University of Oregon. After a hiatus of nearly thirty years, raising a family and pursuing odd jobs, she had a dream about being an inept dragon and began writing in 2019. Her work can be found or is forthcoming in Cirque, Amethyst Review, Humana Obscura, Open: Journal of Arts & Letters, River Heron Review, HerStry, Raft, and The Bookends Review, among other publications. She is also the winner of the PDXToday 2023 Poetry Contest. Kerstin lives in Portland, Oregon.

Slayer (short story)

Benjamin Spada is the author of the award-winning *Black Spear* series of military-thriller novels. Born and raised in California, Benjamin J. Spada has had a lifelong passion for storytelling. Benjamin is a dedicated taco aficionado, self-described "Professor of Batmanology", proud Fil-Am and lumpia enthusiast, and has served for fourteen years in the United States Marine Corps. He has been a Martial Arts Instructor, been assigned as a Section Leader in the Wounded Warrior Battalion for our nation's wounded, ill, and injured, and served overseas to help train our foreign military allies in defense against chemical, biological, and nuclear weapons. He has trained Marines, Sailors, Federal Agents, and other friendly forces in individual survival measures for everything from nuclear attacks to deadly nerve agents. Despite these grim assignments, he has carried on with equal amounts of sarcasm and stoicism. When out of uniform, Benjamin is an avid sci-fi and horror movie fan, tattoo collector, comic enthusiast, and two-time holder of the Platinum Trophy in *Elder Scrolls: Skyrim*.

Editor

H David Blalock has been writing for print and the internet for more than 50 years. He has edited anthologies, collections, and magazines for multiple publishing houses in the US and Europe since 1990. His own writings have appeared in novels, novellas, anthologies, and magazines.

www.ingramcontent.com/pod-product-compliance
Lightning Source LLC
LaVergne TN
LVHW010342070526
838199LV00065B/5775